Skip Shaughnessy

in

The Truth Shall Make You Free

Skip's Action Series

Book 2

Marjorie Strebe

Published by:
Marjorie Strebe
Trenton, OH 45067

Interior Design by Marjorie Strebe
Book Cover Design by 100 Covers

Skip Shaughnessy in The Truth Shall Make You Free / Marjorie Strebe
Library of Congress Control Number: 2024902060
ISBN: 978-1-7372025-8-5
Printed in the United States of America

Then said Jesus to those Jews which believed on him, If ye continue in my word, then are ye my disciples indeed; And ye shall know the truth, and the truth shall make you free.

John 8:31-32

Table of Contents

Chapter 1

A Deadly Shot

Sitting in the briefing room of the Kenton, Wyoming, Police Department, Skip Shaughnessy felt like he didn't belong. Was his perception skewed because of the circumstances that had brought him here from the start? Kenton PD required their officers to be twenty-one years old and, since Skip was only nineteen, he was too young to be with their department. But they didn't know that.

Off in another world, Skip thought of the last time he'd seen his fiancée. They'd spent the day together and he took her on a picnic. Then they went for a walk down by the river. Boy, did he miss her.

It had been a terrific day. Holding hands, Skip and Cassandra had strolled across the concrete bridge. And they leaned against the railing, watching the motor boats fly across the water, leaving a trail of white behind them.

"Skip, do you really have to go?" asked Cassandra.

Skip nodded. "I leave in the morning. That'll give me a day to get settled before I start my assignment."

"Where are you going?"

"I can't tell you."

"When will you be back?"

"I don't know," said Skip.

"How will I get in touch with you?"

"You can't."

"Will you be able to call me?" asked Cassandra.

Skip shook his head. "No, and that's gonna kill me. I'm going to miss you so much."

"Will you be in danger?"

Skip sighed. Boy, did she have a lot of questions. He either didn't know the answer or he couldn't tell her.

"I don't know, Cassie. But undercover assignments can be dangerous. So can police work."

"But, what if you're in trouble? How will I know to pray for you?"

"Just pray for me everyday while I'm gone so I don't get into trouble."

His field training officer, Randy Tidwell, pulled up a chair beside him, jerking him back to the present. "Good morning, Shawn. My wife and I are having a cook-out this afternoon, and you're invited."

"Thanks, Randy. I'll be there." Skip adjusted his dark glasses, which protected his light-sensitive eyes. "Do I need to bring anything?"

"Yeah, bring your girlfriend."

Skip immediately thought of Cassandra. "I would, but I'm between girlfriends right now."

As the briefing got underway, Sergeant Calvin Daley informed the first-shift officers of criminal activity around town, making special mention of the drug problem in the area. Then he dismissed them.

Skip followed Randy out to their police cruiser and slid behind the wheel.

It was the second week of May in 1995, almost seven weeks before Skip's twentieth birthday. He could hardly wait to look older – to *be* older. And his birthday just wasn't coming fast enough.

Randy jumped in beside him, and they turned out of the station parking lot, heading to their assigned area.

"So what were you thinking about in the briefing room?" asked Randy.

Skip glanced at him, then back at the road. "Now what would make you ask a question like that?"

"Because when I walked in, you were in another world. Believe it or not, I said 'Good morning' to you twice before I pulled out the chair and sat down beside you."

"Oh. Well, you know, I was thinking about how bad I need a girlfriend."

9

Randy started laughing.

Just then, a call came over their radio, alerting them to a silent burglar alarm at the Westgate Computer Warehouse.

Randy acknowledged the call before directing Skip on the quickest way to get to the warehouse.

Flipping on his lights and siren, Skip sped through town, code three. A few short blocks from the warehouse, he cut the sirens and coasted to a stop on a silent approach.

The officers exited their vehicle and darted toward the double-glass doors. They peered through the glass into the dark and supposedly deserted building. Skip tugged on the main office doors, but they were secure.

"Let's split up and check the outside perimeter of the building," said Randy. "I'll meet you around back."

Turning back to back, the officers headed in opposite directions, slipping around the side of the warehouse. Skip grasped the knob of the first door he came to, but it didn't budge, so he moved on. He found the second door ajar.

"I found an open door," he whispered into his mic.

"Request backup and stay put. I'll be there in a minute and we'll go in together."

Awakened from a sound sleep, Cassandra bolted upright in bed. It was only 7:12 am, and the house was quiet. Yet, she was overcome with a sense of dread.

Skip!

Without wasting one precious second, she bowed her head and started praying for his safety and protection. She had a feeling that if she didn't pray for him, she might not see him alive again.

A moment later, Randy joined Skip. Not waiting for backup to arrive, the officers drew their guns and entered the warehouse.

"Police!" Skip felt for a light switch, but there was none on that wall.

Randy sighed. "Great. We'll have to search in the dark."

The officers pulled out their flashlights.

"This is the police!" called Randy. "Lay down your weapons and come out with your hands in the air."

Skip crouched behind large boxes, darting from one to the next. his gun in his hand, his trigger finger alongside the barrel of his gun. He scanned the dark warehouse, seeking signs of movement. He listened intently, certain there was an intruder. *Someone had left that door ajar.*

Randy yelled again. "This is the police! Lay down your weapons and show yourselves, and no one will get hurt."

Skip jumped. He thought he saw movement out of the corner of his eye, so he swung his aim in that direction. Ready to fire on the first thing that moved, he kept his finger off the trigger. He wondered how many people they were up against. He had never known anyone to pull a warehouse burglary alone, so there were at least two people involved, but he and Randy could find themselves seriously outnumbered.

With shadows everywhere he looked, Skip started to hyperventilate. If only backup would arrive.

Yea, though I walk through the valley of the shadow of death, I will fear no evil; for Thou art with me. Thy rod and Thy staff, they comfort me.

As Psalm 23 ran through his mind, Skip silently prayed for God's guidance and mighty hand of protection upon him and his partner.

Catching sight of an armed burglar, Skip swung his aim toward the suspect, his finger on the trigger. "Drop it! Now!"

The man threw his left arm up. With his right index finger through the trigger guard, he let his gun sway, prepared to set it on a nearby box.

A gunshot echoed through the warehouse, and a second gunman tumbled off a twelve-foot high steel shelving case. Skip flinched and almost dropped his Glock.

Still holding his gun by the trigger guard, the other burglar twirled it into his hand and shot at Skip. Dropping to one knee, Skip returned fire.

The man jerked. The gun slipped from his grasp and he fell backward.

Skip cringed. He just sent this man into a Christ-less eternity. Not that he could have done it differently.

The light flickered on, and backup flooded the warehouse. Six officers scattered to complete the search. Seeing two dead men lying on the warehouse floor, an officer yelled to Skip and Randy, "You guys wait outside."

Randy bounded to Skip's side. "Shawn, are you OK?"

Skip choked down a lump. He lowered his gun before rising to his feet.

"Man, that was some good shooting." said Randy. "From here it looks like you shot him right through the heart." Randy turned him toward the door. "Let's go."

Skip swallowed a lump that threatened to choke him. Feeling sick to his stomach, he spun around and bolted out the door, his gun still in his hand.

Randy dashed after him. "Shawn, are you all right?"

Re-holstering his gun, Skip leaned both hands against the hood of a police car and took a deep breath, shaking his head.

"It's pretty devastating when you kill someone. You hope and pray that you never have to take someone's life, but to be forced into a shoot-out so early in your career …" Randy's voice trailed off. "Hey, man, I'm sorry."

"Being sorry doesn't change anything."

"No, it doesn't, but what choice did you have? You may be between girlfriends right now …"

Skip wasn't between girlfriends. He was actually engaged to be married, but Randy didn't need to know that.

"… but you still have a family somewhere …"

13

Skip thought of his mother and little sisters.

"... And at the moment you pulled the trigger, it was either you or him, because he intended to kill you."

Skip looked at Randy. "You killed a man, too. Doesn't that bother you?"

Randy rested his hand on his partner's shoulder. "Tremendously. But if I hadn't shot him, he would have killed you. I had the means to stop him, and I took it. Someone was going to die in there. I didn't want it to be you."

Standing upright, Skip wiped his hands on his trousers and glanced at the open warehouse door. Officer Joseph Kowalski led a third suspect out to the police car in handcuffs. He paused to talk to Skip and Randy.

"Three shots were fired. His partners were both killed. He surrendered in a hurry. You guys all right?"

Randy nodded. "Physically."

Joseph patted Skip on the back. "Hang in there, Shawn."

Skip looked at Randy. When he completed this assignment, he would go home to his family because of Tidwell's intervention. He hoped and prayed that Randy wasn't involved with the department's internal corruption. How could he turn in a friend – the man who'd just saved his life?

14

Chapter 2

In Time of Need

Arriving on the scene, Sergeant Daley relieved Skip and Randy of their weapons and transported them back to the station. Leading Skip into an unoccupied office, detectives questioned him about the warehouse burglary and grilled him on every last detail of the circumstances that led to the shooting deaths of the two suspects.

Skip sat at the table with his hands folded in front of him. He struggled to answer their questions calmly, without emotion, but he had trouble keeping his voice from cracking. He killed a man. How could he ever pick up his gun again?

"You're dismissed, Shawn. Chief McNare wants to see you before you go home."

"Yes, sir." Sliding his hands into his pockets, Skip stepped into the hallway and found Randy waiting for him.

"You OK?" asked Randy.

Gazing down at the floor, Skip shook his head.

"You'll feel better in a little while. Let's go home."

"I need to see the chief."

Randy followed Skip down the corridor into the chief's office.

Bryce McNare glanced from Skip to Randy. "I've arranged for both of you to talk to a counselor tomorrow. Tidwell, you've been with us long enough to know the drill. Be here at 10:00 tomorrow morning. Effective immediately, you're both on administrative leave – with pay, of course. Tidwell, you're dismissed. Close the door on your way out."

Leaning against the chief's desk with his legs crossed at the ankles, Skip grasped the edge on either side. He swallowed hard, on the threshold of a tearful explosion, and dropped his gaze to the floor.

"You all right?" asked Bryce. "You're awfully pale."

Skip struggled to get his words past the lump in his throat. He *wasn't* all right. Swallowing again, he shook his head.

"This complicates things. Doesn't it? Have you ever been involved in a shoot-out before?"

Skip shook his head.

"I didn't think so. I'm concerned about letting you go home alone. You're so isolated here. You have no family support in town, and due to the circumstances, you can't call home."

This assignment is turning into a nightmare.

"Talk to me, Shawn. Tell me I'm overreacting and that you'll be all right."

Skip's eyes glistened with tears, and he looked at Bryce. "I killed a man, Chief. Have you ever had to kill someone?"

"Once. And believe me, that was enough. So if it's any consolation to you, I have an idea how you feel. I want you here at 9:00 tomorrow morning for counseling. But if you're not finished by ten, Tidwell can wait. Now, you have my number if you need someone to talk to before then. Promise me you'll call, regardless of the time."

"I'll call."

"You think you'll be all right tonight?"

Skip nodded. "I'll be at Randy's place this evening, so I won't be alone."

"All right, son. You're dismissed."

Skip left the chief's office and joined Randy in the locker room.

"Why did the chief want to see you in private? What did he say to you after I left?"

"To call him if I need to talk. I think he's concerned that I might do something foolish tonight. I told him that I'm gonna be at your place, so I won't be alone. That satisfied him. Why? What's the big deal?"

"Uh ..." Randy crinkled his nose. "Never mind. It's not important."

Skip's stomach churned with an uneasy feeling – a feeling that Randy was involved in something illegal. Desperately hoping he was wrong, he pushed that thought from his mind and changed clothes, turning off

17

the voice-activated tape player and dropping it into his trouser pocket before leaving the station.

He groaned just thinking about the boarding house where he'd rented a room. It was a small, three bedroom, two story brick home that was actually bigger on the inside than it looked from the curb because it wasn't very wide, but it was deep. All the bedrooms were upstairs, and the downstairs was laid out in such a way that a roomy entranceway separated the living room on the left from the staircase on the right. A little corridor to the right of the stairs led to the back door. The dining room was straight ahead past the staircase and the kitchen was to the right of it, tucked neatly behind the stairs with a hallway leading from the kitchen to the back door.

Charlene Davarie, Skip's landlady, distrusted men and hated cops. She only rented to him because she needed the money. Despite the reasonable rent he paid each week, he didn't like living in a hate-filled environment, so he kept to himself as much as possible.

Randy trotted after him. "Hey, Shawn, where are you going?"

"Home, I guess." He had no place else to go.

"I'm going shopping for the groceries we'll need for the cook-out. Why don't you come along?"

"Thanks, Randy, but I need some time alone."

"Well, I'll see you around 4:00 then."

Skip forced a smile. "I'll be there."

Dropping behind the wheel of his dull-red Camaro, a rental car that had seen better days, Skip cranked the engine and headed home. But his mind wasn't on his driving. He replayed the shooting in the warehouse over and over again, wondering what he could have done differently. Why did that man have to die? Strangely, Randy didn't seem bothered.

Not sure how he'd gotten home, Skip entered the house in a fog.

"Shawn! What are you doing here?" Mrs. Davarie barked.

Skip jumped.

"I have company coming – a women's group – and you promised that you would be gone during the day."

Skip was not in a mood to deal with her right now.

"Don't tell me, you got fired."

"I got put on administrative leave." Skip trotted up the stairs to his room.

"Young man, if you disrupt my group in any way ..."

"I won't." Skip entered his room and closed the door.

With a sigh, he rewound the tape from his pocket tape player, switched it off, and deposited it on the nightstand beside his bed.

"Will I ever record anything worthwhile?"

He dropped onto the bed. Removing his glasses, he buried his face in his hands and broke down in tears.

The isolation he'd lived with for the past three weeks, magnified by the shooting death of the burglary suspect, threatened to swallow him whole. They felt like the longest three weeks of his life.

That must be how people in the witness protection program felt – forced to start over – new location, new identity, unable to communicate with family or friends. Everything is left behind. And that was how Skip felt working undercover for the Kenton Police Department. The other officers knew him as Shawn Christopher.

Engaged to be married, he hadn't seen or talked to his fiancée since Chief McNare had brought him in for this job assignment. How Skip craved telephone time with Cassandra. He desperately wanted to hear her voice, to spend time with her, and to be reminded of how much she loved him.

Tears spilled down his cheeks and he looked toward heaven. *Lord, I need help. How do I cope with this?*

The answer came almost instantaneously as God brought Scripture verses to his mind.

Trust in the LORD with all thine heart; and lean not unto thine own understanding. In all thy ways acknowledge him, and he shall direct thy paths.

Thou wilt keep him in perfect peace, whose mind is stayed on thee: because he trusteth in thee. Trust ye in the LORD for ever: for in the LORD JEHOVAH is everlasting strength:

Sliding to the floor on his knees, Skip bowed his head and prayed. "Lord, I don't understand what's happening, but help me to trust You. You could have taken my life when You took my father's, but You chose not to. You could have taken me today, but You didn't."

His heart full of grief over the life he'd cut short, Skip buried his face in his arms, unable to continue. As he grew quiet, the Lord spoke to his heart.

Skip, you did not take that man's life. I preserved yours. He died because he sold himself to sin. He could have surrendered at any time and chosen to live. Instead, he died in his rebellion.

Skip pondered that thought. His mind shifted from the man who died to the goodness of God, His mercy, and His mighty hand of protection. Folding his hands on the bed, Skip prayed for the families of the men who died, for his mom and little sisters, and for Cassandra. Lastly, he prayed for himself.

Lord, help me to obey You. Give me wisdom and discernment to identify the corrupt cops in this department. And the boldness to speak up. Use me in a mighty way.

Wiping his eyes, Skip slid on his glasses, crawled onto the bed, and opened his Bible. With his head propped on his hand, he started reading, but the emotional roller coaster of the morning had left him exhausted. After a while, he laid his head down and closed his eyes.

Chapter 3

Escaping the Crazy

Landlady

A slamming door startled Skip awake, and he bolted upright. The voices in the hallway drifted right through his bedroom door.

"That boy's sleeping! He claims he's on administrative leave and came home from work at 12:15."

"Is that a fancy way of saying he got fired?" asked another lady.

"No," came a third voice. "My nephew is a cop. Administrative leave means that the police department is requiring him to take some time off."

"Why?" demanded Mrs. Davarie. "He only started three weeks ago."

"And he's already on administrative leave? Then either he shot someone or they're investigating him for something."

Skip heard Charlene gasp. "Already? How's he going to tell that poor girl?"

"What poor girl?"

"I found a picture of the prettiest young girl in his room. I suspect she's his girlfriend, but he never mentions her."

Skip had heard enough. Pulling out his suitcase, he started packing.

She's been going through my things, Lord. Searching my room. That picture of Cassandra was tucked under my clothes in my drawer. And she was in my room just now when I was sleeping. I'm not staying here another night.

After neatly packing his suitcase, he crawled onto his bed with his Bible. Skip spent another hour with the Lord, in prayer and in His Word. When he finally closed his Bible, he knew he had personally witnessed the power of God.

God's peace enveloped him, and tranquility replaced the trauma. Although Skip now felt emotionally stable enough to return to work, he first had to be cleared by the court system. And that could take weeks.

I'll think of it as a vacation. What kind of a vacation is this without Cassandra? Lord, I miss her so much.

Please help me wrap up this assignment so I can go home.

Skip looked at his wristwatch. It was past three. He must have slept for quite awhile. Settling at the desk with a sheet of notebook paper and a pen, he jotted his landlady a note that said, *Mrs. Davarie, I've only been an inconvenience to you, so I'm moving on. Shawn.*

Skip drummed his fingers on the desk and glanced around the room. He didn't know where he'd go from here, but anyplace was better than Charlene Davarie's boarding house.

Leaving the note on the desk, he dropped his voice-activated tape player into his shirt pocket. He hoped that at Randy's house, it only recorded a bunch of guys having a good time, but he knew the importance of being prepared. Slinging his navy carry-all bag over his shoulder, he picked up his suitcase and started out the door.

He could hear the laughter and chit-chat of Mrs. Davarie's ladies group coming from the dining room and knew they were gathered around the table. Their noise masked the sound of his departure as he crept down the stairs and through the small corridor that led to the back door. Hiking around the house, he reached his rented Camero, tossed his bags into the trunk, and took off for Randy's house.

"Charlene, tell us about that handsome cop you've taken in as a boarder."

"Please, Jasmine, he was nothing more than a means to an end. I wouldn't have even taken him, except I've heard that several rookie cops are involved with drugs, and I wanted to cash in on it before this guy got caught like the rest of them. But if they're already investigating him, it sounds like I'm a little late."

"Sure does," said Donna.

"So you haven't found anything, yet?" asked Jasmine.

Charlene sighed. "No, and I searched his room thoroughly this morning. I didn't even find a loose nickel, and that's a shame, because he's as crooked as the rest of them."

"Marisa might disagree with you," said Kendra. "She absolutely adores him. She dropped by one day and showed me a photograph of them sitting together at your dining room table. With that blond hair, he could easily pass for her brother."

Charlene rose in anger. "He's been looking at my daughter? I'm setting him straight right now!" She stomped toward the stairs. "Are you ladies coming?"

The other ladies raced after Charlene as she led the charge up the stairs and exploded into Shawn's bedroom. Seeing an empty bed, her glare shot toward the open bathroom door.

"Shawn!" She glanced around the room. "Show yourself this instant."

As the other ladies trailed her into the bedroom, Jasmine picked up a note lying on the desk.

"He's gone, Charlene." Jasmine handed her the paper.

"Gone? What do you mean, *'gone'*?" Charlene snatched the note from her and read it. Tossing it aside, she dashed to the dresser and yanked open the drawers. Finding them empty, she slid open the closet door. "He can't just leave. He still owes me next week's rent."

Kendra raised an eyebrow. "Listen to yourself, Charlene. How can he owe you for *next week's rent?*"

"I need that rent money!" Charlene waved her arms like a wild woman.

"Then maybe you should have treated him with a little more respect and consideration," said Jasmine.

Chapter 4

Baiting the Trap

Sitting in a lawn chair on his back porch, Randy shucked corn on the cob while chatting with his three comrades from the Kenton Police Department.

"Is your wife suspicious about the extra cash you're bringing home?" Calvin tossed a peeled cob into a bucket of shelled corn and grabbed another.

Randy shook his head. "I told her it's a bonus from the PD. How about you?"

Calvin nodded. "Same here. But I can't believe we already have to break in another rookie."

"They caught Menzo in three weeks," said Officer Scott McGuire. "He barely received his first pay-off. What's up with that?"

Tossing a shelled corncob into the bucket, Officer Jarred Jacobs leaned forward in his lawn chair and folded his hands. "What if Menzo fingers us?"

"He won't," said Randy. "His wife is expecting their first. He loves her too much to see anything happen to her or the baby. He'll keep his mouth shut."

Calvin's eyes widened. "Did you threaten them if he ratted on us?"

"Of course not. But I told him that if he said anything about our involvement that we couldn't guarantee the safety of his family. Things happen, ya know."

"We need to back off for awhile," said Jarred. "The next bust might be ours. Chief McNare is getting wise."

"You're paranoid," said Calvin. "The chief doesn't suspect us. He's watching the rookies. Randy, shall we invite Christopher to join the team?"

"I intend to. He has a special bond with the chief, so Chief McNare won't suspect him for quite awhile."

"Well, it's getting too risky. I want out," said Jarred. "I won't tell a soul, but don't drag me into it if you're caught."

"We won't get caught," said Scott. "Our greedy little patsy will take the fall before we do."

"In fact ..." Randy glanced at his watch. "He should be here any time."

When Skip reached Randy's brick, ranch-style house, his double-car driveway was already full of cars. Skip parked his red Camero at the curb and switched on his voice-activated recorder as he stepped from the car. The well-manicured lawn and beautifully landscaped property held Skip in awe. With one hand in his pocket, he strolled up the front walkway and rang the doorbell. A smiling Tracy Tidwell greeted him.

"Come in, Shawn. The fellows are in the backyard shucking corn on the cob. We're just about to fire up the grill."

Skip stepped into the house and glanced around. To the right of the entranceway, lavish living room furniture graced the large front room with expensive paintings decorating the walls. To his immediate left was the roomy dining room with a large glass cabinet, filled with costly china.

Wow! Expensive furnishings on a patrolman's salary. Lord, I hope Tidwell's not involved with the department's internal corruption.

It was one thing to turn in a stranger, but Randy was fast becoming a trusted friend.

"You have a beautiful home," said Skip.

"Thank you. Lately, Randy has brought home some sizable bonuses, allowing me to use the money anyway I'd like."

"Sizable bonuses? Did he say how he earned them?"

"No, come to think of it, he didn't."

"I could use more cash," said Skip. "Maybe he'll let me in on his secret. Where's the back door?"

"Straight ahead and through the kitchen."

Without realizing it, Tracy provided Skip with an opening to casually broach the subject with his partner. How Skip hoped that Randy had earned the money legitimately. He dreaded the thought of turning in a fellow officer, especially after the man had saved his life this morning. And if Randy was involved, Tracy would suffer.

The highly polished hardwood floor led him through the house into the kitchen. Pushing through the back door, Skip stepped onto the patio.

"Good timing, Shawn," said Scott. "You got here after all the work was done."

"What are you talking about? I'm twenty minutes early."

Calvin motioned for Skip to join them. "You look in good spirits, all things considered. How do you feel?"

"Starved! When do we eat?"

The officers erupted into laughter.

"Soon." Randy pulled a beer from the cooler and tossed it to Skip.

Skip handed it back. "Thanks, but I don't drink. You got soda?"

Randy stood and picked up the bucket of shelled corn on the cob. "You bet. We'll take this in to Tracy and grab the platter of meat to throw on the grill. Help yourself to the soda in the fridge."

Skip trailed Randy into the kitchen where Tracy prepared all the trimmings to add to their grilled steaks. Pulling a cola from the refrigerator, his eyes widened at the sight of the expensive meat.

"I paid a bundle for these." Randy leaned against the back door and pushed it open, carrying a large platter of seasoned steaks.

Skip followed him. "May I ask you something? Tracy said that you earned a huge bonus at work. How'd you do it? 'Cause I could really use extra cash right now."

"I earned that money by going above and beyond the call of duty."

"I'll go above and beyond the call of duty."

Setting the tray on the picnic table near the grill, Randy withdrew a sealed envelope from his rear trouser pocket and handed it to Skip.

No, Lord, not Randy. Anybody but Randy.

He glanced at the other officers who gathered around him when he tore open the envelope. With a gasp, he emptied a stack of one-hundred dollar bills into his hand.

"Wow! There's at least two grand here."

"Twenty five hundred dollars, and it's yours. Now you can move out of that dumpy boarding house and rent yourself a nice place like I have."

"But I haven't earned this."

"You will. Consider it an advance on your first bonus. Are you in?"

"I'm in!" Skip slid the envelope into his back pocket. "What do I do?"

Lifting the lid to the grill, Randy lobbed the steaks on one at a time. When they hit the hot rack, they sizzled. "The department makes some good drug busts. What we're doing ..."

"We? Who else is working with you?" asked Skip. Now that he had Randy talking, he intended to glean as much information as possible.

"Calvin and Scott."

Skip glanced at Jarrod, who had quietly excused himself and was entering the house.

That's odd that Randy invited him to the cookout when he's not involved. But then, I'm not involved. Randy must have invited Jarrod for the same reason he invited me – to draw us both into his illegal activity. Only Jarrod refused to get involved.

Sitting down at the picnic table, Randy looked up at Skip. "Our mission is relatively simple. We target drug dealers, arresting them and getting loads of drugs off the street. Then the department rewards us with a percentage of the dough we confiscate."

Calvin nodded. "It's a win-win situation. The PD recycles eighty percent of the drug money into the department for the purchase of much-needed equipment, and we get a bonus for making the bust."

Skip was impressed. *Good plan. That even sounds legal.*

"We'll put you in charge of the money," said Calvin with a grin.

So I take the fall. Nice guys.

But Skip had to look excited, so he imitated Calvin's grin. "You trust me that much?"

"We do," said Randy. "I've ridden with you for the past three weeks, and I know that you can be trusted."

If you only knew.

"After the bust, you set aside twenty percent and log down the rest as recovered drug money," said Calvin. "After work, we all meet at Scott's house. You bring our bonus money, and we'll split it evenly among the four of us."

"When's the next drug raid going down?" asked Skip.

"We're working on it. It takes awhile to gather the information needed to make a good bust," said Randy. "But I have a great informant. We tip him well for the information he provides."

"Don't worry," said Scott. "We'll keep you in the loop."

Randy lifted the lid to the grill and flipped the steaks.

Skip glanced toward the house. *Poor, Tracy. She has no idea that Randy is involved in something illegal. Lord, I can't do this to him. What will happen to her?*

Chapter 5

A Tough Decision

When the Tuesday afternoon Bible study concluded, Crystal Masterson, the oldest of triplets, bowed her head while Tim Brock closed in prayer. Then, munching on cookies and discussing the lesson, the young people straggled out. Tim's roommate, Danny, and the triplets remained behind.

"How's everything going at home?" asked Tim.

Jayme Jade Masterson, known to her sisters as JJ, tossed her long black hair over her shoulder. "*Terrible!* Dad doesn't want us attending your Bible study."

"Why not?" asked Danny.

"He says you're filling our heads with a bunch of garbage," said Billie, the youngest of the triplets. "He thinks religion is for the weak. We're Mastersons. No Masterson gets weighed down by religion."

"Did he forbid you from coming?" asked Tim.

Crystal shook her head. "Not yet, but it's coming."

"What about your mom?" asked Danny. "Is she saved?"

"No, but she's not giving us grief about it like Dad," said Crystal. "I think if Dad got saved, she would too."

Billie and JJ nodded in agreement.

"Let's pray for them again," said Tim. "God can get hold of their hearts in ways we could never imagine. His resources are unlimited."

Although the youth group had just prayed for them, the girls bowed their heads and Tim led. "Lord Jesus, our hearts are heavy with concern. Please allow the girls to attend Bible study. Move on their dad's heart in a way that only You can. Send someone he'll listen to, and open his eyes to the Truth. In Jesus' name, Amen."

"Thanks, Tim," said Billie.

"Hey, would you girls like to go skating with us tonight?" asked Danny.

Crystal sighed. "I can't go. Tonight is my wedding party." She turned to her sisters. "But you two don't have to be there."

Billie grabbed her arm. "You don't mind?"

"No. If I could, I'd join you."

"Shall we pick you up about seven?" asked Danny.

The girls shook their heads. "Better not. We'll meet you here," said Billie.

Bidding their friends goodbye, they headed home. Their father was waiting for them when they entered the house.

"Didn't I forbid you from going to that religious gathering?" he demanded.

"No!" They spoke in unison.

"Well, I'm forbidding you now. You've brought all the religion into this house that I intend to tolerate."

"Dad, you don't understand," said JJ.

"I don't want to understand. I've allowed this to go on far too long. I thought this was a fad you'd outgrow as quickly as you were afflicted, but I can see I've been mistaken."

Crystal said, "No, Dad, it's not a fad. It's ..."

"Worse than a disease!" finished Carl Masterson. "Now, you will sever your relationship with those two religious fellows. What are their names? Tim and Danny?"

"You don't even know them!" cried Billie.

"I don't want to know them. They're not fit to be seen with a Masterson. I fully expect you girls to stop associating with lower class citizens."

Without waiting for a response, he whirled around and stomped off. The girls stared after him. Once their father was out of sight, Crystal motioned for her sisters to follow her upstairs. She had a plan.

Having recorded sufficient incriminating evidence, Skip sought an opportunity to return to his car. He needed to put away the tape player so it didn't

39

accidentally fall out of his shirt pocket. That would be a disaster.

Everyone hustled in different directions. While Randy plucked the steaks off the grill, the others helped Tracy set the picnic table, haul food outside, and retrieve drinks and condiments.

Slipping out the front door, Skip trotted to the Camero and deposited his pocket tape player in the glove box of the car, returning as quickly as possible. No one even missed him.

The thought of turning in his fellow officers left him dizzy with doubt. Randy had saved his life this morning. Is this how Skip repays him? By causing him to lose his job and go to prison? Yet, his integrity was on the line.

These men are breaking the law. And my department sent me to identify the officers involved in the corruption. Skip sighed as he followed the others into the backyard. *This will be hard to do, Lord.*

Accustomed to listening to the voice of God, Skip had no trouble hearing God's response. *Doing what's right isn't always easy.*

Seating himself at the picnic table, Skip bowed his head and thanked God for the food. Prayer before mealtime was an ingrained part of his routine. The others sat respectfully quiet until he'd finished.

"Hey, Shawn, we didn't know you were a church boy." Scott glanced nervously at his partners.

Uh, oh. I'd better come up with something fast. "I always pray before I eat, and boy did I have a lot to thank God for today."

"You're talking about that healthy bonus, I presume?" asked Calvin.

"You bet."

The other officers grinned and noticeably relaxed as they piled their plates full of food. Quickly accepted as part of the group, Skip enjoyed the camaraderie that the meal initiated, all the while feeling like a traitor.

The side gate swung open and two teenage boys bounded into the back yard.

"Food!" exclaimed the older boy.

Without being invited, they grabbed plates and started filling them up.

"I thought you guys were at the park playing basketball," said Tracy.

"We got hungry," said the younger lad.

Oh, great. This decision will also affect two kids.

God spoke to Skip's heart. *The consequences of sin can be far-reaching.*

But Tracy and the kids will suffer tremendously, Lord.

Indeed, they will. Randy's decisions have hurt his family.

Skip glanced around at the other officers as they laughed and joked throughout dinner. *What about my decision to turn him in?*

Skip, sometimes it's hard to do the right thing.

"Hey, Shawn, did you hear me?" Randy snapped his fingers in front of Skip's eyes.

Skip jumped and looked at him. "I'm sorry. I was lost in thought. Did you say something?"

"We decided to play poker after dinner. You want to play?"

These guys were dishonest, and he didn't like the atmosphere they created. So he had no desire to stay any longer than necessary. That would dramatically increase his discomfort. It was time to leave.

"Thanks, Randy, but I'm gonna take off. I don't gamble anyway."

The others stared at him.

Calvin scrutinized Skip, a lighted cigarette in his hand. "You don't drink. You don't smoke. You don't gamble. You don't cuss. You pray before you eat. You go to church. I suppose you even read your Bible."

Skip took a last swig of soda and tossed the empty can in the trash can. "My, my. You talk about those things like they're all bad. Yeah, I read my Bible. There's a verse in Luke that says, 'Ask and it shall be given you.' So I asked God for more money, and Randy gave me $2500 in cash and the opportunity to participate in this great bonus program. And I have no intentions of losing it in a poker game – *not to anybody.*"

Returning from the house with the cards, Randy rested a hand on Skip's shoulder. "Relax, Shawn. We understand."

Sitting on the bench, he tipped the cards out of the box and started to shuffle them. Calvin and Scott shoved things aside to make room for their card game.

Skip stood. "Let's help Tracy clear the table and put away the food before I leave and you guys get involved in a card game."

Jarred stacked the dirty plates. "I agree, Randy. Your sweet wife has fed us a number of times, and we always abandon her with the cleanup. Let's show her how much we appreciate her by lending a hand today."

Randy, Scott, and Calvin looked at each other when Skip and Jarred started clearing off the picnic table. Tracy offered an appreciative smile as she loaded the dishwasher with the dishes they brought her. Begrudgingly, the other three officers pitched in to help. In fewer than ten minutes, the work was done and the officers sat down to play cards.

"Well, gentlemen, I have something to take care of, so I need to go." Skip stepped into the house to thank Tracy for having him over. Then he took off for Chief McNare's house, praying for courage to do the right thing.

Chapter 6

A Change in Plans

Ushered into the chief's house by a teenage girl, Skip waited on the living room sofa.

"Shawn, are you all right?" Chief McNare hurried into the living room. "Angela told me that you were here. How are you holding up?"

Skip looked at the chief, but he couldn't shake the images of Tracy and her boys. He dreaded this.

"You look like you're still in a state of shock. This morning's shoot-out affected you tremendously."

"The shoot-out?" Skip brushed his hand through the air. "That's history. I spent the morning with the greatest counselor available. His name is Jesus. I'm here because of this." Skip pulled the miniature tape player from his pocket and rewound the tape.

Chief McNare grimaced. "Is this what I think it is?"

"Yes, sir." Skip passed him the envelope of cash.

Bryce emptied the envelope into his hand and whistled. "Is it Tidwell?"

Skip nodded. "I don't want to hurt his family, but ..." His voice trailed off and he looked away.

"Tough decision, huh, son?"

"You have no idea. And Randy wasn't working alone." Skip pressed play on the recorder.

The Masterson mansion bustled with activity while servants prepared the ballroom for the massive wedding party to be held that evening. Crystal knew that her mother would oversee every facet of the planning, attending to the dozens of last-minute details in an effort to put together a perfect evening.

Perfectly boring. This is my party and they won't even allow me to invite my friends. I would have invited our entire Bible study group.

Come evening, the triplets crept down the wide, spiral staircase and slipped out the front door.

"Did anyone see us leave?" asked Jayme.

"Are you kidding?" said Crystal. "The house is so chaotic right now, you won't be missed for hours."

With teary eyes, Billie grasped her hand. "Thanks, Crystal. I hate disobeying Dad, but even he would agree that we owe Tim and Danny a face-to face good-bye."

Jayme nodded. "We'll be home in about an hour. Thanks for covering for us."

Skip sat still, allowing Chief McNare time to digest the information on the tape.

Expelling a frustrated sigh, the chief just shook his head. "Oh, man, it's worse than I thought. I suspected Tidwell was involved, although we couldn't prove it. But Calvin? Skip, don't feel badly about turning them in. They were setting you up to take the fall."

"I know."

The chief held up Skip's pocket tape recorder. "May I keep this? I don't have anything small enough to play that tiny cassette."

"Sure. I bought it for this assignment anyway."

"I'll see that you're reimbursed."

"Well, sir, it's been a long three weeks. And when you confront these guys tomorrow, I have no desire to be there. I already feel like a traitor."

"You know you'll have to face them in court."

Skip nodded. "But I can't bear to see them handcuffed and taken to jail with the evidence that I provided for you, especially Randy. Is it all right if I head home?"

"Tonight?"

"Right now. I'm anxious to see my fiancée."

Chief McNare studied him. "I have never talked to an officer so young who demonstrated such peace mere hours after being involved in a shoot-out, especially when someone died. You won't need counseling tomorrow."

"Then I'm free to go?" Withdrawing his wallet, Skip removed his Kenton police shield and photo ID card.

Bryce took them from Skip. "I guess you won't need these any longer. I'll call Captain Kramer and inform him that your assignment here is through."

"I'll call him. I want to call home anyway. Sir, about my administrative leave..."

Chief McNare passed the cordless telephone to Skip. "Sorry, son, that's not my call. You know this shooting will go before the Grand Jury to determine that it was justifiable before you may return to work, and that could take several weeks. Inform your captain of the situation. I'll get with him next week to fill him in." Bryce stood and grasped Skip's hand. "Now, if you'll excuse me, my son's waiting to finish our chess game."

The chief disappeared around the corner. Telephone in hand, Skip started to punch in his home phone number and stopped. Disconnecting, he set down the phone.

I'll be home in ninety minutes anyway. I'll surprise everyone.

Chapter 7

The Beginning of Trouble

Carl Masterson's shiny black Lincoln Continental jerked and thumped.

Great, thought Billie.

JJ glanced around. "What's that noise?"

Thumpity ... thumpity ... thumpity

Struggling to maintain control of the car, Billie let up on the gas and coasted onto the shoulder of the road. "I think we have a flat tire."

"A flat!"

The girls slid from the vehicle and hurried around the car, examining the tires.

"Wonderful," moaned JJ "We must have picked up a nail or something. I wonder if there's someplace we can call Devon."

Billie shook her head. "Doesn't look like it. Dad's going to kill us." She eyed the gleaming white pickup truck that veered to the side of the road. A tall, muscular man jumped out, strutting toward them. "But let's hope someone else doesn't do it first."

The man whistled. "Looks like you two beauties are in a slight predicament."

"You wouldn't mind changing our tire for us. Would you?" asked JJ hesitantly.

He winked at them. "Suppose I just give you a lift to my place. Then you can use the telephone to call for help."

As if that would really happen. Billie forced a smile. "Thanks, but we have help coming. We just thought if you changed our tire, we could get back on the road a little quicker."

"Suit yourself." The man jumped back into his truck and took off.

His vehicle had barely disappeared from view when a two-door sedan, weaving all over the road, jerked to a stop a few feet from them and a short, round man stumbled out. He almost fell over staggering toward them. The girls separated and dodged him.

"Come with me, gorgeous." He lunged toward Billie.

Billie leaped aside. "I can't leave my sister here alone. Something bad could happen to her."

"She can come, too." The drunk staggered toward JJ.

JJ evaded him. "Now would that be fair? There are two of us and only one of you."

The drunk stopped. "Hm. I guess that could be a problem. I'll go get my best friend. Then you can both come." Staggering back to his car, he drove away.

Oh, no, he's actually going to get a friend. Lord, send someone to help us. I can't believe we've gotten ourselves into this mess.

"Billie, I'm scared. Let's pray that God sends help before that lunatic returns with his companion." Holding hands, the girls bowed their heads and prayed.

They had scarcely said 'amen' and opened their eyes when a sports car coasted to a stop directly behind them. Blinded by the headlights, the girls stepped behind their dad's Lincoln, studying the handsome blond driver. He was dressed in pleated navy trousers and a pressed white dress shirt. Despite his enticing smile and sharp dress, dark glasses hid his eyes, and that unnerved Billie.

"Would you ladies like some assistance? It looks like you're stranded."

Exchanging glances, the girls eyed him skeptically, not certain that he was any more trustworthy than the riff-raff they'd already encountered.

He strolled toward their vehicle. "Let me change your tire, and I'll have you back on the road in about fifteen minutes or so."

JJ reluctantly opened the trunk. "You'd change our tire in dress clothes?"

Lifting the tire out of the trunk, he examined it. With a frown, he dropped it to the blacktop. Billie's heart sank when it didn't bounce. "Well, I was going to, but your spare is flat."

"Flat!" cried JJ. "Oh, no."

He replaced the tire in the trunk and closed it. "May I offer you a lift somewhere? I don't want to leave you stranded. It's not safe, especially this hour of the night. I'd be glad to give you a lift home or drop you off at a friend's house."

The girls sighed and looked at each other.

"My name is Skip Shaughnessy." He offered them his hand.

Reluctantly, Billie grasped his hand and gazed intently into his shaded eyes. "Skip. Is that a nickname?"

"No, Ma'am, it's my given name. My nickname is Shawn."

"Shawn," said JJ. "I've simply got to know. Why are you wearing sunglasses at night?"

"My eyes are hyper-sensitive to light, and the headlights of on-coming cars practically blind me."

That satisfied Billie.

"Thanks for the offer," said JJ. "But you're going the other way."

"I'm in no hurry." Skip strolled back to his car.

Billie drew closer to her sister. "He's cute, and we're stuck."

"I know, but we don't *know him,* Billie. How do we know he'll take us home?"

"We prayed for God to send someone to help us. Didn't we? He's the third guy who's stopped and the first one who even offered to change our tire. And that last guy was drunk. If we stay here or try to walk someplace safe to call Devon from a pay phone that drunk guy might come back with a friend. Then we'll *really* be in trouble."

JJ nodded. "You're right."

The girls started toward Skip's car. Approaching headlights illuminated the entire street, making them squint. Swerving from side to side, the small sedan slid to a stop near them. The doors flew open, and two men staggered out.

"Hey, gorgeous. I brung my friend, just like I said I would. Now you won't have to fight over me. You'll each have your own man."

Billie cringed at the thought. "Thanks, but we decided to go with him."

The man looked at Skip. "There's only one of him." He swayed, struggling to maintain his balance. "I think." He studied Skip for a moment. "Yep, that's what I thought. There's only one of him. And there's two of us, so you'll want to come with us."

He reached for JJ, but Skip tripped him. The girls scrambled back, and the drunken man tumbled to the asphalt.

"Hey, you did that on purpose," said his friend.

Clenching his fist, he swung at Skip. Skip ducked. The man swung at him again, and he stepped aside. The other guy staggered to his feet and lunged toward him, swinging wildly. Skip jumped back, dodging the men as they attempted to gang up on him. The girls screamed and scrambled into his car.

Seizing one man by the arm, Skip twisted it behind his back and tripped him. He tumbled into his comrade, and they both toppled to the blacktop. While the drunks struggled off each other, Skip calmly slid into the car and made a U-turn.

53

"Boy, can you fight," said Billie.

"I'm a purple belt in karate, but it didn't matter. Those guys are so drunk, they couldn't hit each other. Now, where am I going?"

"We live on the outskirts of Laramie," said JJ.

"I'll run you all the way home and make sure you get there safely."

"Thanks. My name's Billie and this is my sister, Jayme, but we call her JJ."

"I'm pleased to meet you."

The girls chatted softly, stopping long enough to give him directions to their house.

"This is quite a drive."

"That's for sure," said JJ. "We appreciate you going out of your way to take us home because we couldn't have walked it."

Finally, Skip pulled through a gate and started down a long, winding driveway toward the Masterson estate. His mouth dropped open. "Is this where you live?"

"Uh-huh. You like it?" asked JJ.

"Wow! It's incredible!" Mesmerized by the mere sight of the massive estate, he slowed the car to a stop.

Almost immediately, the girls jumped out. They were still quite a hike from the house with no lights to illuminate that part of the drive. That could work to their advantage, enabling them to slip back into the house unnoticed.

Billie sighed. She knew that Devon would gladly go get the car, change the tire, and repair the spare without their father ever knowing his Lincoln had been moved.

Yes, everything will work out just fine.

Hearing a car door open, she glanced back. Skip had stepped from the car.

"Hey, you needn't jump out here. You've still got quite a hike. Let me run you all the way to the house."

"Thanks for protecting us back there, Shawn," said JJ. "We appreciate it more than you'll ever know."

"And for the lift home," added Billie. "But we can walk from here."

The girls started their long hike up the driveway.

Skip called after them. "Not in the dark by yourselves. If you insist on walking, then I'll walk you all the way to the house."

"That's not necessary," said Jayme.

Billie grinned. She was delighted to have him escort them all the way to the door.

Skip reached into the car and cut the engine. The headlights automatically switched off, leaving them in the dark.

Squealing tires pierced Billie's heart with an instant dread. Caught in the glare of blinding headlights, she dived out of the path of a speeding car. JJ screamed, followed by the dreadful sounds of crunching metal and breaking glass, which snuffed out the light. Billie leaped to her feet and the sisters ran into each other's arms.

The driver's door slowly opened, and Crystal stepped from her dad's Cadillac. Her hand covered her mouth in shock as she studied the wreckage.

"Oh, Lord. I can't believe I did that." She buried her face in her hands. "Are you two all right? I almost ran over you. I'm so sorry."

Billie and JJ gasped. The girls struggled for words, but they wouldn't come.

"Who's car did I demolish?" asked Crystal.

Her sisters hurriedly glanced around. Skip lay unconscious on the concrete, surrounded by broken glass.

Chapter 8

Hiding the House Guest

Jayme went cold inside. *Oh, Jesus, what have we gotten ourselves into this time?*

Crystal gasped when she saw Shawn. "What have I done?" Her sisters dashed around the car and squatted beside him.

"He's breathing," said Billie.

"Oh, my gosh! What do we do?" Jayme fought back the tears. "We can't call an ambulance. The publicity would be devastating."

"Crystal, where were you going in such a hurry?" asked Billie.

"To find you. The party started ten minutes ago. Mom and Dad said they fully expected you two to be there. So I called Tim's house. He said you never got there. I shouldn't have been speeding, but I was scared something had happened to you."

"We had a flat," said Jayme. "Shawn started to change it for us, but the spare was also flat, so he brought us home. Oh, man, Dad's gonna kill us."

"Yeah, he is," agreed Billie. "But this guy helped us." She drew in a deep breath. "OK, JJ, you stay with Skip. I'll run in and get Devon. He'll know what to do. Crystal, you'd better get back to your party before Mom and Dad get suspicious. If they ask where we are, tell them we're still dressing."

Crystal nodded and raced Billie to the house.

Tears spilled down Jayme's cheeks. *Lord, we've gotten ourselves into such a big mess, and we desperately need wisdom to do the right thing. I pray Shawn will be all right. Protect him from dad's wrath. Dad will have him arrested.*

Billie returned with Devon Phelps, the tall, dark-haired butler.

"I called the doctor," Devon said. He squatted next to Shawn and touched his face. "He's warm and breathing. What happened? Who is this boy and why's he here?"

"Oh, Devon." Billie and Jayme collapsed in his arms sobbing.

When Doctor Zeimbah arrived, the two men rolled Shawn onto a backboard, careful to keep his head, neck, and back aligned. Lifting the board, they hauled him up the never-ending driveway and into the house. The girls followed them to the doctor's first floor office where they had had all their childhood checkups. They waited in the

58

hallway while he examined Shawn. Finally, he stepped out to talk to them.

"He looks pretty good, considering. I don't think he sustained any broken bones. No back or neck injury that I can tell."

"He'll be all right, then," said Jayme.

"It's uncertain. He suffered a pretty hard blow to the head, and we won't know what kind of damage it caused until he regains consciousness ... *if* he regains consciousness."

The girls gasped. "If?"

"I suggest you call an ambulance and have him transported to the hospital. They're far better equipped to deal with this kind of injury than I am on a house call. And he really should be x-rayed for internal injuries. Who is he, anyway?"

Jayme thought fast. "He's our brother!"

Billie's eyes widened in shock. "Brother? Oh, yeah, our brother."

"Not with that blond hair," said Doctor Ziembah. "He doesn't look a bit like you girls."

"So show us in the baby manual where brothers and sisters always look alike," said Jayme.

Devon raised a curious eyebrow but remained silent.

"I didn't know you had a brother," said the doctor in surprise.

"Well, now you know," said Jayme. Cramming trembling hands into her pockets, she rocked back on her heels. "He was away at military school."

"Yeah, that's right," agreed Billie. "But don't tell Mom and Dad he's here. It's a surprise. They weren't expecting him home until next week."

Doctor Ziembah eyed them skeptically. "All right. I won't say anything. But if he's really your brother, that's another reason you should get him to a hospital. Goodnight, all." The doctor graciously excused himself and headed for the front door.

With weary sighs, the girls looked from Shawn to Devon.

Billie blinked back tears and slowly sat down on a nearby chair. "Maybe he's right," she said. "Dr. Ziembah is one of the best doctor's I've ever known. Devon, maybe you should call an ambulance."

Devon shook his head. "No. I've been thinking, they never just send an ambulance. They'll send the police, too. When they see these two wrecked cars, they'll start asking questions. They'll want to talk to your dad. And when your dad sees this boy, he's as good as dead. It would be better if you and your sisters told your dad what happened on your own terms. So let's just keep him here for now, and you can find a way to tell him after the party."

Devon called for two of the servants, instructing them to change Shawn into clean pajamas and move him to a third-floor guestroom. Then he left the house with Shawn's car keys in his hand.

The girls dashed to their rooms to change. Billie hurried down the stairs to make an appearance at the party and Jayme ran upstairs to sit with Shawn. They were afraid to leave him alone.

About fifteen minutes later, Devon entered Shawn's room with a suitcase in his hand. "I found this in the trunk of his car. That boy was going someplace. Now, Missy, tell me what *really* happened? You girls don't have a brother, so who is this lad?"

Jayme buried her face in her hands. Looking up at him, she swallowed hard and gave him a brief run-down.

"Devon, please don't tell Dad. He's forbidden us to see Tim and Danny because they're not rich. He said their not worthy to be seen with a Masterson. But Billie and I don't care that they're not rich. We like them for who they are. We don't want Mom and Dad to do to us what they're doing to Crystal – forcing her to marry some guy she doesn't love just because he's wealthy. What can we do?"

"There's only one thing to do," said Devon. "You'll have to tell your parents the truth."

"You won't cover for us this time?"

"How? I can go get the Lincoln and change the tire. We can clean up the mess in the driveway, but how do we keep your father from finding out about those two wrecked cars?"

Jayme groaned.

"And how do you plan to keep this boy hidden? You know I'd never rat on you, and the doc is gone for the night, but what happens when this lad regains consciousness, or worse yet, he slips into a coma?"

"I don't know." Jayme was trying not to think about that. "I guess we'll have to tell Dad."

"Well, dear, you do what you must. I'll send someone for the Lincoln and clean up the mess in the driveway. We can't have it blocking our guests when they're ready to leave."

Jayme forced a smile. "Thanks, Devon. You're a real friend."

As Carl Masterson's head servant, Devon had been with him for fifteen years and was well-respected among the Masterson family members, as well as the household staff. But none of them appreciated him like the triplets.

Devon had cared for them from the time they were toddlers. Often called upon to baby-sit, he read them bedtime stories, assisted with their homework, stood in for their parents at school conferences, attended their school programs, and cheered at their soccer games. But more than all that, when they got themselves into a scrape, Devon always found a way to rescue them from their father's wrath. This mess was too big for him to patch up.

Devon left, and Jayme sat next to Shawn on the full-sized bed. Wetting a clean cloth in cool water, she folded it and placed it across his forehead. Despite the broken glass fragments that he'd fallen onto, he sustained few cuts, but his golden-blond hair didn't hide the nasty bruise on the right side of his head.

"Billie's right," said Jayme. "You are cute." With a grin, she caressed his arm.

The door opened, and Billie rushed in. "I'll sit with him, JJ. Dad's getting suspicious that he hasn't seen you."

"How does he know I'm the one who's missing?"

Billie laughed. "Good question. Must be the color of your gown. You'd better make an appearance at the party."

With a heavy sigh, Cassandra tossed her novel on the coffee table. An avid reader, she could lose herself in a romance within minutes. But ever since Skip left, she couldn't seem to focus – not on her novel, not on a movie, not on a conversation, not on the task at hand – not on anything.

And every time she picked up her book, she only re-read the same dramatic scene over and over again. After reading it every day for three weeks, she practically had it memorized. Caroline just found out that her steady wasn't so steady as she thought because he had another girlfriend on the side.

Cassandra frowned. *Skip's been gone for three weeks. He could have found a way to call me if he really wanted to. I'll bet he's with another girl right now!*

The girls took turns sitting with Shawn during the party.

Shortly after eleven, Devon hastened in. Seeing the beautiful young lady on the bed next to Shawn, his mind flew to the advice he'd given her awhile ago and knew she hadn't taken it. If the girls had confessed to their father, something would have happened by now, and with Carl Masterson's temper, it would have been something unpleasant. It may not hurt to offer a gentle reminder that they needed to tell their dad he now had a house guest.

"Did you tell him?" he asked.

"Tell who what?"

"Your dad. You said you were going to tell him what happened tonight."

"Oh, Devon! Did JJ or Billie say they were going to tell Dad? I've got to stop them. Stay with him, will you?"

Oops, that's Crystal. "Wait, Missy! I can't. I have to ..."

Crystal dashed off without listening. Devon gazed down at Shawn. He hadn't moved.

"There's something that Mr. Masterson wants done right now," he said. "You should be OK unattended for a short while." Devon left the room and closed the door.

As head of the staff, Devon oversaw staff duties, which kept the household running smoothly. Tonight, he tended to details of the wedding party and ensured that the guests had their needs met.

Crystal raced down the stairs to the ballroom and stopped just outside the door. She took a deep breath to compose herself, then entered the room slowly and gracefully. Immediately, she cornered her sisters. "Have either of you told Dad what happened?"

"No, why?" asked Billie.

"Don't tell him yet. I was thinking of ..."

"Oh, there you are!" exclaimed Martha Masterson. "Where have you girls been? The party is practically over, and we've hardly seen any of you all evening. Now I fully expect all three of you to stay the rest of the evening."

"But Mom ..."

"No buts. Now, mingle with the guests for awhile."

The triplets looked at each other as she walked away.

"Great," said Crystal. "I left Shawn with ..." She suddenly felt light-headed when she spotted Devon across the room. " ... Devon! Oh, no, he's alone!"

"He'll be OK," said Billie. "He's been out for hours. What are the chances of him waking during the short time he's alone?"

JJ's eyes grew misty. "The doctor said he might not wake up at all."

Chapter 9

The Search is On

He turned his head and opened his eyes, straining to bring his surroundings into focus.

What happened? The bright over-head light made him squint, so he shaded his eyes with his hands. *W-where am I?*

He slowly sat up, glancing around the fancy room. Throwing off the covers, he scooted off the bed and stumbled to the closed door. He opened the door and poked his head out, squinting as he looked up and down the deserted hallway.

"Hello? Anybody here?"

Despite blurry vision, extreme fatigue, a pounding headache, and light-headedness, he quietly closed the door behind him and wandered down the hall looking for someone. *Anyone.*

He entered rooms through one doorway and exited through another. His legs hurt, making it difficult to walk as he limped down hallways and labored up and down stairs. He roamed aimlessly through the massive estate until he was hopelessly lost, but he didn't cross paths with another person.

"I'm going to check on Skip," said Billie. "If Mom asks about me, tell her I ran to the ladies' room, and I'll be right back."

Billie slipped out the door and up the stairs. When she reached Skip's room, his bed was empty, and her heart skipped a beat. Despite the doctor's grim prognosis, he *did* wake up, but where was he? She dashed from his room, conducting a brief search for him.

"Skip? Skip, where are you?"

Not finding him quickly, she returned to the ballroom for reinforcements.

Gripped with fear, JJ and Crystal hurried from the ballroom to help their sister find Skip. They couldn't risk him stumbling into either of their parents, especially their dad. He would have Skip arrested and charged with burglary or breaking and entering, even stealing the pajamas he wore, without asking any questions. Despite the trouble they'd be in, the girls couldn't let that happen. They had to find him before their dad did.

Congregated outside his room, Crystal spouted off instructions. "Billie, check the rooms down that hallway.

JJ, cover all the guestrooms. He may have gone into the wrong one. I'll check the storage rooms. He couldn't have gone far."

"What do you mean?" gasped Billie. "He's been alone for forty minutes. He could be anywhere in this house by now."

"Then we'd better get busy and find him before Dad does, or worse, he inadvertently stumbles into the ballroom during the party!" said JJ.

"What's wrong?" Devon hurried down the hallway toward them.

The triplets jumped.

"Sorry to startle you, but I've been trying to catch up with you ladies since you left the ballroom."

"Shawn's gone," exclaimed JJ. "We've got to find him before Mom and Dad do."

Devon nodded. "Indeed, we do."

I should have stayed in bed. The boy touched his throbbing head. *The more I move, the worse my head hurts. How come I don't know where I am? I don't remember this place at all.* He studied his surroundings. *In fact, right now I don't remember much of anything.*

Overwhelmed by fatigue and light-headedness, he leaned against the wall to calm his pounding head, blinking and rubbing his eyes, trying to clear his blurry vision.

I have to lie down. He glanced up and down the hall, squinting and shading his light-sensitive eyes. *Which room did I come out of?* Everything looked the same.

Staggering down the hall, he pushed open a bedroom door. *Here it is.* Too exhausted to cross the room to the bed, he leaned back against the door, closing it as he slid down to the floor. His eyes dropped shut and he lay down on the plush carpeting, up against the door.

As the wedding party moved into the late evening hours, Carl and Martha Masterson noticed that the attendance in the crowded ballroom had dwindled.

"Where is everybody going?" asked Martha.

"Not everybody. Just the servants."

"The girls are gone, too."

"Hm." Carl stroked his chin and looked around for Devon, but he had disappeared as well. "Stay here, dear. I intend to find out what's going on." Striding into the hall, he flagged down one of the servants hurrying past.

"Yes, Mr. Masterson."

Making circles with his hand, Carl indicated the continuous activity. "What's going on, Todd?"

"Going on, sir?"

"Yes. Going on. You're supposed to be tending to the needs of our guests. Not running around out here. So would you like to tell me what's going on?"

"Um ... W-We're looking for someone."

"Who?"

70

"I don't know."

"Then how will you know if you find him?" asked Carl.

"Oh, I'll know. He won't be dressed for a party."

"Who initiated this search?"

"Devon."

Carl raised an eyebrow and motioned for Todd to carry on. "Now I'm curious. I think I'll join the search party."

When Carl didn't return to the party, his wife and future son-in-law, Michael Andrews, went looking for him. Too obvious to ignore, the guests noticed that people were disappearing one at a time.

"What's going on? Where's everyone going?" asked a young lady.

"Let's find out," said a young man.

The party dwindled to a few unconcerned guests who didn't care what was happening outside of their own conversations. The rest wandered into the halls to find out what was going on. As word of the search circulated, most of the guests joined in.

"What are we looking for?"

"A missing boy."

"Is he little?"

"No. We're looking for an intruder, possibly armed and dangerous."

"Don't be ridiculous. He's wearing pajamas."

"So he's a fruitcake. He must have escaped from a mental hospital."

Unnerved by the chaotic hunt for Shawn in which nearly everyone had enlisted, Devon felt the turmoil and now feared for the boy's safety. The spreading rumors caused confusion among the guests.

Finally, Carl called a meeting at the bottom of the stairs, gathering together as many folks as possible. Standing on the fourth step, he addressed both servants and guests.

"I need everyone to calm down. We have an unconfirmed report of an intruder. That's all I know. He may or may not be armed, so I recommend the ladies return to the ballroom where they'll be safe."

"How will they be any safer there?" called a man from the crowd. "I suggest we call the police?"

Devon shook his head and slowly backed away from the crowd. "That poor boy. We have to find him before this mob does."

Chapter 10

The War Begins

At a loss to know where Shawn could have wandered and anxious to find him before their father did, Crystal suggested they expand their search to cover the second floor.

Billie raised an eyebrow. "You suppose he went into one of our rooms by mistake?"

"Probably not, but this house is so big, he easily could have gotten lost and ended up on the second floor without realizing it."

"Well, which room is directly under his?" asked JJ.

"Crystal's!" said Billie. "It makes sense to check her bedroom."

The girls hurried down the stairs and rounded the corner to their bedrooms. Crystal's bedroom door was closed, as always. She doubted Shawn was in her room, but it didn't hurt to peek in. Turning the knob, she pushed, but the door wouldn't open.

"That's funny. It feels like it's locked, but the knob turns." Crystal rattled the knob and leaned into the door with all her strength. "It's stuck."

Her sisters helped her, pounding and pushing on the closed door. Between the three of them, they finally forced it open. The girls filed in and flipped on the light. Sitting on the floor behind the door, Shawn slapped his hand over his eyes.

"Skip!" Billie dropped to her knees in front of him. "We've been going crazy looking for you."

Shawn shaded his eyes and looked at her. *My name is Skip?*

JJ and Crystal knelt on either side of him.

"I'm sorry. I got l-lost. When I finally found my room again, I was too tired to make it to the bed."

Crystal placed a warm hand on his left shoulder. "This isn't your room, Shawn. Your room is upstairs."

She saw the confusion in his eyes and the wheels in his mind turning. Striking him with such force may have caused more damage than a few bruises and a simple headache.

Shawn. That girl called me 'Shawn.' But the other one called me 'Skip.'

His whole body ached as if he'd taken a serious tumble, but he didn't remember falling. Bruised and sore,

74

he brought his right hand to his throbbing head, closed his eyes, and massaged his temple, struggling to remember what had happened to him.

Oh, man, do I hurt. Especially my head.

A soft hand rested on his right arm. "Are you OK?"

Swiveling his head to look at her, he did a double take, looking from one girl to the other. They looked nearly identical. *Twins.* "Who are you?"

"Jayme. Shawn, you gave me and Billie a ride home this evening." She motioned toward the girl kneeling in front of him. "Don't you remember?"

Still squinting, he shielded his eyes from the blinding light and shifted his gaze from girl to girl to girl. His head swam.

No, this can't be. Now I'm seeing three of them.

Closing his eyes tightly, he leaned his head against the wall, hoping that when he reopened them, all the extras would be gone.

"Shawn, you remember giving us a ride home. Don't you?"

With his eyes still closed, Shawn shook his head.

"We've got to tell Dad what happened. It's our fault he got hurt."

"We can't tell Dad! Do you know what he'll do to us?"

Shawn cracked open his eyelids and peeked out at the girls arguing over him. There *were* three of them. He wasn't imagining it.

"My gosh, Crystal, do you know what he'll do to Shawn if we don't speak up?"

"OK, we'll tell him, but only if we have no choice," said Crystal. Come on, Shawn. Let's get you back to your own room."

The girls helped him to his feet, steered him out the door, and nearly into the arms of their surprised father.

"Daddy!" chimed the triplets.

Shawn shook his head and struggled to focus, but everything was still blurry. The man seized his arm and jerked him away from the girls supporting him.

"Devon, call the police!" he ordered.

"Carl!" yelled another man, who shoved his way through the noisy crowd that was gathering around Shawn and the triplets. "We caught him in Crystal's room, and all you can say is *'Call the Police'*?" Clenching Shawn's shirt, the guy slammed him back against the wall. "What did you do to Crystal?"

Ouch. Shawn grimaced when his throbbing head smacked the wall. With his eyes squeezed shut, he instinctively threw his arms in front of his face to protect himself from an imminent blow.

Still clasping Shawn's shirt, the man shook him violently. "Answer me! What did you do to her?"

With this guy yelling at him and the crowd of people all talking at once, the noise level rose a decibel. Shawn clamped his hands over both ears to drown out the commotion.

Crystal cringed as she watched her father's rage explode on Michael. Yet, because of the party guests, she thought he might actually be maintaining an element of self control.

"Let him go, Michael," commanded Carl. "This is a problem for the police."

"Not till he tells me what he did to Crystal."

"Stop it!" screamed Crystal, attempting to force herself between Shawn and Michael. "He hasn't touched me!"

Michael shoved her aside. "You're lying, Crystal! Quit protecting this scumbag."

"That's enough!" yelled Carl. "*I* will take care of him! You have *no business* interfering with how I handle things in my own house. Now let him go before I call the police on *you*!"

With a vice grip on Shawn's right arm, Carl yanked him away from Michael.

His head spinning, Shawn lost his balance and tumbled into the crowd of on-lookers. Carl jerked him to his feet and Michael wrenched him up by his other arm.

"Release him, Michael!" commanded Carl.

Securely held between the two men, being yanked back and forth, Shawn felt like the rope in a game of tug-of-war. With every sharp movement, his headache intensified. His head swimming, noise and light momentarily faded into oblivion.

Shawn trembled and his legs almost buckled out from under him. A sudden jerk on his left arm brought him back to full consciousness.

"Stop!" he hollered. "Please. I didn't do anything. I didn't do anything."

Chapter 11

The Drama Unfolds

Devon observed the crowd of guests clustered in the hallway as the drama unfolded before them.

"Why, he's just a kid, maybe seventeen years old," said a middle-aged man in a black business suit.

"He is wearing pajamas," whispered another.

"He doesn't look dangerous to me," said a young, red-headed woman.

"No, he doesn't." Most agreed.

Shaking his head, Devon jostled his way through the crowd to reach Carl and Michael, on the verge of pulling Shawn apart, if they didn't clobber each other first.

"I'll pulverize him for bothering Crystal!" Releasing Shawn's left arm, Michael drew back his fist, prepared to belt him.

"No!" wailed the triplets in unison.

Crystal lunged at Michael and grabbed his arm. "Don't, Michael. Leave him alone!"

Michael shoved her so hard, she tumbled into Billie and they both toppled to the floor. Devon seized the angry young man and dragged him away from Shawn. Rushing to his aid, Tyler and Zack, two of his staff members, restrained Michael.

He struggled to break their hold. "Let me go!"

Clutching Shawn's arm, Carl glared at Michael. "Is this how you intend to treat my daughter after you're married?"

"She's lying to protect him, Carl!"

Carl pulled Shawn close. "Crystal's guilty of a lot of things, but lying isn't one of them. None of them lie. *None of them!*" Carl turned to Devon. "Did you call the police?"

"No, Mr. Masterson. The boy is innocent. Involving the authorities could open the door to ..." Devon's voice trailed off. *A lawsuit.* But the crowd didn't need to hear that, and the girls had not told their dad what had happened, yet.

Carl narrowed his eyes and scowled at Devon. "Could open the door *to what?*"

To Devon's relief, he didn't wait for an answer. He continued without the slightest pause.

"He has no business being here. I intend to press charges against him for breaking and entering, trespassing and burglary. And that's just the beginning. I will prosecute to the full extent of the law. Now, *go call the police.*"

"Sir, involving the authorities is not wise. I assure you, he's innocent."

"And how would you know that?"

With all eyes on him, Devon glanced at the girls and read the fear on their faces. Silence settled over the crowd, and the triplets held their breath. For him to answer Carl's question, meant he had to betray their confidence, and he wasn't about to do that. "I'm sorry, sir. I'm not at liberty to say."

"Then you're not at liberty to keep your job. After tonight, you may consider your employment terminated."

"No!" cried Crystal. "Don't fire Devon. He was only protecting us. We didn't want you to know what we did." She burst into tears.

Her sudden outburst caught her father by surprise. "Crystal, get hold of yourself, and tell me what this is all about." Carl turned to Devon. "Have Kenny escort our guests back to the party."

Devon knew that the guests wanted to hear Crystal's explanation, but no one dared try Carl Masterson's infamous temper. Speculating in hushed voices, the crowd returned to the ballroom, leaving the Mastersons alone with Shawn, Devon, and a still-restrained Michael.

Crystal looked at her father. "Right before the party started, I jumped into the Cadillac and took off to find JJ and Billie."

"JJ and Billie? Where did they go?"

Gazing down at the floor, Jayme shuffled her feet. "We went to see Tim and Danny."

"After I forbade you to see them again?"

Jayme nodded. "I'm sorry, Dad. You've always taught us that it's proper to give that kind of news in person, so we went to tell them good-bye. That's all. But we never got there. The Lincoln blew a tire, and we got stranded."

Billie stepped closer to her father. "Dad, this is Skip. He stopped and started to change the tire for us, but the spare was flat, so he brought us home. He was headed the other direction."

"How did he get in the house?"

Crystal wiped her teary eyes. "Devon and the doctor brought him in after ..." She choked on her words. "... after I hit him with the Caddy. I'm sorry, Dad. It was dark out, and I didn't see him, and ..."

"My goodness, Crystie. *You hit him with the car?*" Immediately, his eyes glazed over with fear, and Devon knew that the word *lawsuit* had raced through his mind. Carl tightened his grip on Shawn's arm and glanced at Devon, unable to hide his concern.

Pasty white and trembling, Shawn brought his free hand to his head. "Sir, may I please sit down?"

Michael struggled against the men who restrained him. "That still doesn't explain what he was doing in Crystal's room!"

"No, it doesn't." Carl turned to Shawn. "Young man, what were you doing in Crystal's room?"

"Crystal's room? I'm sorry. I thought it was my room."

Carl raised an eyebrow. "Your room?"

"He's lying!" said Michael.

"No, he's not," said Billie. "Why must you accuse everyone else of lying?"

"What's your name?" demanded Carl.

"Sir?" Shawn swayed.

Devon shook his head at the way Carl required him to stand for such trivial questioning. He prepared to move quickly if the boy collapsed, which he expected to happen at any moment.

The young man pondered Carl's question. "Skip? Shawn? I don't know."

"You don't know your name?"

"No, sir."

"His name is Shawn," said Jayme.

"No, it's not. Shawn is his nickname. His first name is Skip. That's what he told us when he picked us up," said Billie.

"Skip what?"

The girls looked at each other and shrugged.

"Um ... he told us his last name," said Jayme. "But we can't remember it."

Carl turned to Shawn. "What about your address and telephone number?"

Shawn blinked and shook his head like he was trying to wake up. "I ... I don't know it."

"He's lying, Carl!" exclaimed Michael. "He's playing dumb and intends to use that car accident as a means to sponge off your wealth."

"That's ridiculous!" snapped Devon. "Doctor Ziembah thoroughly examined him and said he sustained a serious blow to the head."

"Wonderful," moaned Carl. "He has amnesia."

"It does appear that way, sir."

Shawn wavered like he might pass out, but Carl kept a tight grip on his arm. With fire in his eyes, he turned on Michael. "If you touch this boy again, I'll have you arrested." He nodded for Tyler and Zack to release him.

Michael shoved the men away from him and stormed down the hall.

"I apologize, Devon," said Carl. "I reacted hastily in terminating your employment and would like you to continue in my employ."

"Thank you, sir. I would like that very much."

"I assume you've already assigned this lad a guest room."

Devon nodded.

"Very good. Post a guard outside his door. He's not to leave that room without an escort with him at all times."

"Yes, sir."

"Go through his pockets and belongings to see if he has any identification. I'll be in my study, trying to figure out what to do with him. The rest of you may return to the ballroom. Our guests will wonder what's become of us if everyone disappears."

"Come on, son." Devon grasped Shawn's left arm and slid his right arm around his waist for support. Finally, Carl released Shawn's right arm.

Kenny had just returned from escorting the guests back to the ballroom when Devon motioned for him to join them. He hustled up beside them and took hold of

Shawn's right arm. Together they helped him up the stairs, to his room, and back into bed.

"How rested are you?" asked Devon.

"Why?"

"Mr. Masterson wants his door guarded through the night."

"To keep him in or to keep Michael out?"

"To keep him from wandering unescorted through the manor."

"I can do it, but then I'll be useless tomorrow. Why don't you ask Mr. Masterson about posting a guard first thing in the morning? He won't get up again tonight. He's wiped out."

Devon nodded. "I suppose you're right. But keep guard until I clear your suggestion with Mr. Masterson."

Devon searched Shawn's trouser pockets, locating a black leather wallet in mint condition. Thumbing through it, he pulled out money and a driver's license while Kenny rummaged through his suitcase.

"Nothing in here but clothes, hygiene supplies, and a Bible." Kenny refolded everything and arranged it neatly.

Devon headed toward the door. "I'll be back." Hustling down the hallway, he trotted down the two flights of stairs. When he arrived at Carl's first-floor office, his employer was on the phone.

"He has blond hair and blue eyes, medium build, approximately six feet tall. I'd guess he's only about seventeen. My daughter says his name is Skip...I agree. It isn't a common name, so you should easily recognize a missing person's report on this lad."

Devon handed Carl the driver's license he found in Shawn's wallet.

"Oh, wait, Sergeant, he did have ID on him. His name is ..." Carl raised an eyebrow. "... Shawn Christopher? Maybe 'Skip' is a nickname ... OK, I appreciate it. We'll keep him here for now. Bye."

Carl hung up the phone. He slammed the driver's license on his desk and looked up at Devon. "He lied! He told the girls that his name is Skip."

"Sir, maybe it's a misunderstanding. JJ said his name is Shawn. I doubt he showed her his driver's license, so he must have introduced himself."

"Yes, but Billie is convinced that he told them 'Shawn' is a nickname, and his given name is 'Skip.' Yet, his driver's license plainly says 'Shawn Christopher.'"

"Billie must be mistaken, Mr. Masterson. You know how forgetful she can be at times."

"True." Picking up the license, Carl studied it. "Was this all you could find?"

Devon nodded. "Yes, sir. Kenny searched his suitcase thoroughly."

"Suitcase? He was going someplace? Boy, that's just great. Well, the Laramie police have no missing person reports on anyone matching his description, but they'll keep their ears open."

"Sir, his driver's license gives a Forest Valley box number."

"Forest Valley?" Carl re-examined the boy's driver's license. "That's almost two hours away. What would this kid be doing so far from home?"

"I don't know, but maybe we could call the Forest Valley police."

"Good idea, Devon." Carl grabbed the phone and dialed the Forest Valley Police Department. After a brief conversation, he shook his head and hung up.

"No luck?" asked Devon.

"Afraid not. The officer even looked him up in the phone book, but there is no listing for a Shawn Christopher."

"You didn't think to ask him about the name 'Skip'?"

"His name is Shawn Christopher. Why would I waste my breath on a supposed nickname?" Propping his elbows on his desk, Carl buried his face in his hands. "Devon, for some strange reason, I have a feeling that our young guest won't be reported missing."

"So what are you going to do with him?"

Carl shook his head. "I don't know. I *just* don't know."

"Is it crucial to have a guard posted at his door all night?"

"Probably not. Is Kenny with him now?"

"Yes, sir."

"Tell him to be there by 7:00 a.m."

Chapter 12

Searching for Answers

Cassandra was still sitting on the living room sofa when the front door opened and her younger sister, Melanie, entered the house with a big grin. She turned and waved at her friends before closing and locking the door.

"Where were you?" asked Cassandra.

"The movies. That was a great picture."

"Who'd you go with?"

"Probably no one you know. I just went with some of the girls from my class in school. Why?"

"Do any of them happen to know Skip?"

"Are you kidding? They all know Skip," said Melanie. "And when we all get together, he's usually our topic of conversation."

"Why is that?"

"You know perfectly well. Cause we envy you. We all have a crush on him. He's handsome. He's kind. He's easy to talk to. You know all this, Cassandra."

Cassandra sighed and a tear trickled down her cheek as she considered what he might be doing right now. "Yeah."

The warehouse was dark. Shawn crouched behind large boxes and drew his gun. He listened intently, certain there was an intruder. Someone had left that door ajar! His adrenaline was pumping so hard, he was having trouble breathing.

At the sound of two consecutive gunshots, he jumped and pulled the trigger.

"Shawn, are you OK? You shot him right through the heart ... the heart ... the heart."

Shawn bolted upright in bed, breathing hard. Sweaty and trembling, he looked around at his safe and quiet surroundings. *What a nightmare!*

He squinted and looked around the sun-lit room. The dark glasses on the nightstand beckoned to him, so he slipped them on.

Much better.

His heart still racing, Shawn swung his legs over the side of the bed. He grimaced at the constant ache in his muscles.

Oh, man, what happened? Why am I so sore, and where am I?

He studied his unfamiliar surroundings. The events of the night before assaulted his mind like a nightmare come true. He remembered waking up in this room and wandering through a mansion looking for someone who could answer his questions ... being falsely accused ... threatened, yelled at, and fought over.

Fear gripped him. He was still here – a place he obviously wasn't wanted – a place he didn't want to be.

Slowly standing, Shawn massaged his throbbing left leg and surveyed the room. A black canvass suitcase sat on a chair in the corner.

Is that mine?

A suitcase didn't fit in with the room's lavish decor. It didn't belong there any more than he did, so it had to be his. Hobbling over to it, he rummaged through the clothes, selecting navy dress slacks and a short-sleeve plaid shirt. He dressed and tied his shoes.

"I like these." Shawn regarded his reflection in the mirror. "They're comfortable, and I look nice."

Wondering if he dared leave the room, his growling stomach propelled him toward the door, but he stopped when he heard voices out in the hall.

"Hey, Kenny, did Mr. Masterson call the police about that kid yet?"

"Yeah, he called them last night."

"Boy, I wouldn't want to be in his position. Mr. Masterson doesn't take kindly to uninvited guests."

"That's for sure," said Kenny.

Shawn swallowed hard and slowly backed away. He stepped over to the window and peeked out. *Too high. I would never make it to the ground safely.*

While he debated a way of escape, a soft knock rattled his bedroom door. Shawn jumped and spun around to face the door, but he remained silent.

"Shawn?" called a feminine voice through the closed door. "Are you awake?"

When he didn't answer, the door inched open and three beautiful girls with flowing black hair and sapphire-blue eyes gracefully entered the room. With his back to the wall near the window, Shawn couldn't retreat another step. The girls gathered around him.

"How do you feel, sweetie?"

Shawn studied them warily. His stomach rumbled and grumbled, but he recalled last night's incident – their dad's intense anger and hostility toward him just for being there. He didn't know what had brought it on, and he feared a second confrontation.

With a warm smile, one of the girls grasped his left hand. "Come eat. Breakfast is ready, and everyone is waiting for you."

Despite the gentle pull on his hand, Shawn stood fast. He wasn't sure he was invited.

"Skip, we apologize for last night." Another girl looped her left arm through his right. "Dad sent us upstairs to call you for breakfast. A hard, fast rule in this house is that no one eats until everyone is at the table. Dad and Mom are downstairs at the table waiting for the four of us. You don't want to see his anger again. Do you?"

Shawn's eyes widened. "N-n-no, miss."

The triplets escorted him downstairs to the dining room, and Kenny detoured to the kitchen. Although sore, Shawn discovered that the more he walked, the less he ached. Reaching the dining room, he opened the door for the girls. The triplets smiled at him.

"Thank you, Shawn."

"This boy's a gentleman."

"Something you don't see much of anymore."

Shawn smiled and reluctantly stepped into the room behind them. He froze when his shaded eyes met Carl's warm brown ones.

"Have a seat, son. My name is Carl Masterson and this is my wife, Martha. You've already met our daughters – Crystal, Billie, and JJ."

The girls each slipped up a hand at the mention of her name, and this time Shawn noted who was who. They looked nearly identical, but they weren't, and he caught the subtle differences.

"You may consider yourself part of the family for now," said Carl.

I don't think so. He slid onto a nearby chair. Immediately, Jayme and Billie plunked down on either side of him. *Last night he was ready to throw me into prison, and this morning I'm part of the family? He doesn't want me here. I don't like it here. I don't know what brought me here. I have no reason to stay. But I am hungry. I'll eat first.*

As the breakfast foods were passed around the table – biscuits, gravy, ham, hash browns, bacon, sausage, eggs, and fruit – the family conversation centered around the planning of Crystal's wedding and the triplets' upcoming senior year of high school. Shawn served himself and ate quietly, relieved that they ignored his presence.

"Shawn, are you always this quiet?" asked Martha.

Swallowing hard, Shawn glanced around the table. Now the focus of attention, he was forced to interact to avoid being rude.

"I ... I don't know."

"How old are you?" she asked.

Shawn bit his lower lip and looked away. *I haven't any idea, but how do I say that without sounding like a complete idiot?*

"According to his driver's license, he's twenty-one," said Carl.

"Twenty-one!" echoed the triplets in unison.

"No way!" exclaimed Billie. "Skip, are you really that old?"

"His name is Shawn," said Carl.

"No, Dad, it's Skip," insisted Billie.

"His driver's license says it's Shawn. So you will call him Shawn. Is that understood?"

"Yes, sir."

"Do you like the food?" Martha asked him.

"Yes, ma'am, thank you." Shawn finished eating and slowly stood.

Carl studied his attire. "You're dressed nicely, son. Are those clothes from the suitcase?"

"Yes, sir."

"Well, the suitcase and everything in it belongs to you."

Shawn gazed uncertainly at Carl. This morning, he exhibited a calmness that reminded Shawn of the stillness of nature following a devastating hurricane.

As everyone rose from the breakfast table, Kenny rejoined them, and Devon escorted Michael into the room.

"Sir, Mister Andrews is here."

Michael glanced around the room and scowled when he spotted Shawn.

"Good morning, Michael," said Martha.

"Yeah, good morning," he grumbled. "What's *he* doing here?"

"What do you care?" asked Carl. "He's not your problem."

"If he even looks at Crystal, then he becomes my problem, and I'll beat the daylights out of him!"

Chapter 13

Forced to Fight

Shawn looked from Carl to Michael. Between Carl's violent temper and Michael's violent threats, Shawn knew he had to get out of there.

Everyone eyed Michael with amusement.

"Son, you're not the physical type." Carl chuckled at him and strolled away. With grins and giggles, the rest of the family followed.

Michael glared at Shawn, tapping an unlit cigarette in the palm of his left hand.

"Not in the house," said Kenny. "You know Mr. Masterson's rules."

Dropping it back in the box, Michael shoved the package of cigarettes into his shirt pocket. "Ah, I'll have a smoke later."

With a full stomach, Shawn decided that he no longer had a reason to stay. He hobbled through the dining room door and glanced from the huge, winding staircase over to the ultra-wide front door, debating whether he should collect his things and haul his suitcase out the door with him. But where would he take it? He had no place to go. Why lug a heavy suitcase around? It would only slow him down from going no place.

"Are you listening to me?" Michael shoved him with such force that he tripped and fell, but Kenny caught him.

"That was uncalled for," said Kenny. "Now leave him alone."

"Don't waste your jealousy on me," said Shawn. "I don't even know Crystal."

His left leg throbbing, he limped toward the front door. Kenny trailed him. Pulling open the huge door, Shawn stepped outside onto the monstrous front porch with marble steps and concrete pillars.

He turned and spoke to Kenny. "You're under orders to stay with me, aren't you?"

"Yes, I am. The house is quite large and as you have already discovered, one can easily get lost."

Shawn forced a smile. "I did discover that. I don't know what brought me here, but based on Mr. Masterson's reaction to me last night and his comment just now, referring to me as a 'problem,' I know I don't belong. Thank him for me, would you?"

"Thank him?" Kenny cocked his head, obviously baffled.

"Yes, sir. For feeding me, giving me a place to sleep last night, and for not pressing charges against me. I appreciate his kindness."

Shawn hobbled down the stairs and started his long hike down the never-ending driveway. Suddenly aware of someone behind him, he jumped aside. Michael lunged for him and nearly took a nose-dive to the concrete. Regaining his footing, he swung at Shawn with all his might. Shawn ducked.

"You big baby!" Michael swung at him repeatedly. "Get over here and fight like a man."

Shawn evaded him, repeatedly dodging Michael's fist.

Michael kicked at him, but Shawn caught his leg and shoved him backward. The man crashed to the concrete.

Anxious to escape, Shawn attempted to dash around him, but Michael bounded to his feet and clenched his shirt with both hands.

Forced to fight, Shawn raked his fist down Michael's arms, breaking his hold with such force that he pulled the man into him. Seizing his left wrist and elbow, Shawn twisted his arm behind his back and tripped him, shoving him to the ground face down.

With no warning, two servants seized his arms and dragged him away from Michael. Michael scrambled up and backhanded him across the face, sending his glasses flying before slugging him in the eye.

"What a coward you are!" Shawn struggled against the men who restrained him. "Hit me when I can't defend myself."

"You wait until Carl finds out that you attacked me!" Michael clenched Shawn's shirt and shook him. "You'll go to jail!" He drew back his fist, prepared to throw another punch.

Shawn fought to break away from the two servants, but they held him tightly. Allowing them to support his weight, he lifted his feet off the ground and drove them into Michael's midsection.

Gasping for breath, Michael dropped to his knees, doubled over, his arms wrapped around his stomach.

Shawn's feet crashed to the pavement. With his arms still restrained, he slammed his right fist into the groin of the servant on his right. With a scream, the man released him and fell to the pavement in agony. Shawn crossed his right foot in front of his left and smashed his left fist into the groin of the other servant with similar results.

"Goodbye, gentlemen." Limping around the three men, he left them groaning on the concrete driveway and picked up his glasses. He examined them for damage, then slid them back on his nose. "Have a nice day."

Fearful that someone might stop him from leaving, Shawn took off down the long driveway and out the gate, frequently glancing behind him. Despite his sore left leg, he ran for nearly two miles before slowing to a walk.

Finally alone – really alone – he searched his memory for the faintest glimmer of his identity. A sudden fear gripped him. Where could he go? He had no idea where he was or where he belonged. His mind changed direction when he recalled the three men that he single-handedly incapacitated.

How did I do that? Mr. Masterson will be furious that I beat up his servants and his daughter's boyfriend. If he exploded on me just for being in his house, I don't want to be around when he finds out what I did.

Shawn jumped when a car pulled up beside him.

The driver lowered his window. "Need a lift, son? This is an awful lonely stretch of road to be stranded on."

"Thank you, sir, but I can walk."

"You sure? I don't normally pick up strangers, but you look kind of lost. I'm on my way to the Laramie police station and would be glad to give you a lift."

"How far is it?"

"Oh, about ten miles."

"Could you drop me off when you get into town?"

"Sure. Hop in."

Shawn slid into the car and fastened his seat belt. He accepted the ride so he could rest, but he didn't want to get near a police station for fear they might be looking for him. He suspected that Mr. Masterson had already reported him to the authorities.

The driver glanced at him and back at the road. "What happened, son? Did you get caught in a fight?"

"Is it that obvious?" Shawn gingerly touched his tender left eye where Michael belted him.

"Afraid so. That black eye is nasty. Even your dark glasses don't hide it, and the discoloration has spread to your cheek. Maybe I should run you to the hospital."

"I'm all right." Shawn changed the subject. "Is that a police scanner?"

"Sure is?"

"Do you keep it on all the time?"

"Whenever I'm driving."

Shawn chatted with the driver all the way into town. If he directed the discussion, the man wouldn't be asking him questions that he couldn't answer.

Arriving in town, the driver pulled over to the curb and Shawn jumped out. "Maybe I shouldn't let you out here. I don't have a good feeling about dropping you off just anyplace. Let me take you all the way home."

Take me all the way home? Where's home? Shawn's winsome smile belied his turmoil. "Thanks for the lift, sir. I'll be fine." He spoke with an assurance he didn't feel.

"All right, son. Take care of yourself." The man waved and pulled away from the curb.

Shawn looked around. He was in town. Now what could he do?

Jamming his fists into his pockets, he strolled down the sidewalk, gazing into store windows while considering his predicament. He had no money, no means of support, no family or friends, nowhere to go. And he expected the police to come after him. Then he'd go to jail.

Jail!

The fear of the unknown brought on by his memory loss paled in comparison to the horror of serving jail time.

Chapter 14

In Search of Truth

In his office, Carl worked feverishly to complete last month's expense account – business paperwork that he'd set aside to oversee the success of his daughter's wedding party.

The big day was set for the weekend following her high school graduation. He knew she didn't love Michael, but in time she would learn to love him. Regardless of her feelings, he needed to secure her financial future. Not that he was in a hurry to marry her off, but Michael had proven himself to be a sharp and shrewd businessman. His financial success meant that Crystal would never have to work a day in her life, and he didn't want her to miss this opportunity. Hopefully, he could secure Billie's and Jayme's financial futures in the same way.

A sharp knock rattled his closed office door. "Come in!"

The door opened and Kenny poked his head in. "Sorry to disturb you, sir, but we have a problem."

"Where's Shawn? I gave you strict orders that he was not to be left alone for any reason."

"Yes, sir, that's the problem. He said he didn't belong here. He asked me to thank you for your kindness, and he left the house."

Carl jerked to his feet. "He did what?"

"He took off."

"Come on, Ken."

They raced to the front door and met Michael staggering in, holding his stomach.

"What happened to you?" asked Carl.

Michael gagged. "He ... he ... he kicked me."

"Who?"

"Sh-Shawn. He's w-worse than an animal. He ... He attacked me outside. He left G-Grant and Levi in agony."

"Where are they?"

"Out ... outside."

Flinging open the front door, Carl skipped down the marble steps and partway down his driveway where his two servants lay groaning, their hands protecting their groin area from further assault. Kenny hurried after him.

Carl raised an eyebrow and looked back at Michael, leaning against a concrete pillar slightly hunched. "Shawn beat up all three of you without any provocation?"

Michael nodded and started down the steps, shuffling over to join them, but Kenny looked doubtful.

"Where is he now?" asked Carl.

"He took off, and you should be glad."

As Levi dragged himself to his feet, Kenny grasped his arm and helped him up.

"You all right?" asked Kenny.

Levi groaned, barely able to talk.

Jayme and Billie trotted down the marble steps, joining the others in the wide driveway.

Jayme's eyes darted from Levi to Grant. "What happened? Should we have Devon call an ambulance?"

"Grant, do you need an ambulance?" asked Carl.

"No, sir." Grant slowly sat up. "I ... I ... I think I'm OK."

"Good. Would you like to tell me what happened now?"

Michael scowled at Carl. "I told you what happened! If you had a thread of decency, you'd call the police and have that scumbag arrested!"

"What scumbag?" asked Jayme.

"That bum that's been staying here."

"Are you referring to Skip ... Uh, I mean Shawn?" asked Billie.

"You know I am. He's nothing but a no-good freeloader. Amnesia nothing! You've all been duped."

"And you claim that he attacked you unprovoked." said Carl.

"Claim nothing! I have two witnesses."

"That's hog wash!" cried Billie. "Skip ..." Billie shook her head. "Sorry, Shawn wouldn't attack anybody. Last night, he protected JJ and me from a couple drunks. They swung at him several times. He never struck either one of them."

"Billie, why didn't you tell me this last night?" asked her father.

"Sorry, Dad. I guess, I forgot."

"He attacked me!" hollered Michael.

Kenny spoke up. "Maybe so, but you tried to pick a fight with him before he even left the house, and I stopped you. His response told me that he's not easily provoked."

Carl stroked his chin, considering all sides to this fiasco. He knew and trusted Michael, but his respect for Kenny's judgment, combined with the story his daughter shared, cautioned him not to react too hastily. Maybe his servants could provide a more detailed account.

Carl turned to Grant and Levi, both now on their feet. Their pallor and the way they stood hunched indicated that they were still in pain.

"Did either of you see him attack Michael?"

Grant leaned down, hands on his knees. "No, sir. When we got here, Shawn already had him on the ground in a hammer lock. We yanked him off Mr. Andrews."

"Then what happened?"

"Mr. Andrews ..."

"Shut up, Levi!" said Michael.

Levi glanced at Michael, then back at Carl. "...slugged him."

"While you had him restrained?" yelled Carl.

"Yes, sir."

Carl gave Michael a hard look before turning back to Levi. "After Michael belted him, you released him to defend himself. Didn't you?"

"No, sir, we held him tight. We were afraid of what he might do to Mr. Andrews if we let him go."

"So you held him while Michael hit him." Carl turned on Michael. "And you think *he* should be arrested?"

Jayme said, "By the way, Michael, Shawn knows how to fight. He's a purple belt in karate."

Billie skimmed the landscape. "Dad, we got to find him."

"Let him go," scowled Michael. "Now, he's not your problem anymore."

"Unfortunately, you're wrong, Michael. *My* daughter hit him with *my* car on *my* property. That makes him *my* responsibility." Twirling around, Carl Masterson hurried to his Lincoln Town Car. "Come on, girls. He couldn't have gotten too far on foot."

Jayme and Billie jumped into the car to help their father search for Shawn.

Not knowing which direction he'd headed, Carl turned toward town. Within fifteen minutes they'd reached the city limits. When they didn't spot him along the way, Carl guessed that he probably headed the other direction, but since they were already in town, they stopped by the Laramie Police Department. The police could alert all law enforcement officers in the entire county to be on the lookout for him.

Entering the police station at a trot, Carl and his daughters stepped up to the desk.

"Hello, Carl." Sergeant Kinkade greeted him. "What can I do for you?"

"I'd like an all points bulletin put out on a young fellow by the name of Shawn Christopher. It's important we find him."

"Is he lost?"

"More like a runaway."

"How old is he?"

"Twenty-one."

"I'm sorry, Carl. He's of legal age. Did he break any laws?" asked Sergeant Kinkade.

"No, he has amnesia. He was staying with us while we located his family, but he got in a fight with my future son-in-law and took off. He has no money on him, no place to go, no means of transportation, and no memory of his identity. It's imperative we find him."

"Give me his description."

"Six feet tall, 165 pounds, blond hair, blue eyes, dark glasses, wearing navy dress slacks, a short-sleeve plaid shirt, and black leather walking shoes."

"Hey, you described the boy I just gave a ride to," said another officer.

"Jim, you saw him?" asked the sergeant. "Where'd you let him off?"

"LaBonte Park, and I felt uneasy letting him out there. Somebody had already pounded him, and he looked so lost and vulnerable. I offered to take him all the way home, but he wouldn't let me."

"That's because he has amnesia and doesn't remember where he lives," said Carl.

Jim snapped his fingers. "I knew it. I should have followed my instincts and brought him to the station with me."

"Put out an APB on him right away," said Sergeant Kinkaid. "Give this information and description to dispatch. Get it out now, and be sure to include his last seen location."

"Right, Sarge."

Chapter 15

On the Run

Cassandra lay awake in bed, pondering on what Melanie had told her the night before. She knew that Skip was popular with the girls. Would he be able to resist temptation while on this assignment? He hadn't called her since he'd left, but then, he told her that he wouldn't be able to call her.

I wonder why. I mean, who would know if he called me?

She had to talk to her mom. Jumping out of bed, Cassandra ran down the stairs to catch her mother before she left for work.

"Hey, Mom, can I talk to you for a second?" asked Cassandra, hurrying into the kitchen.

With a cup of coffee in her hand and the newspaper open in front of her, Mom sat at the small round kitchen table. "Sure, what's on your mind."

"It's about Skip. I'm worried that some girl will turn his head while he's on that assignment. He attracts girls like flowers attract bees."

Her mother laughed. "Well, I guess that's one way to put it. And he can't help it, because they see in him what you see in him. But I guarantee you, he doesn't see in them what he sees in you. And that's the difference. So you have nothing to worry about."

"Then why hasn't he called?" asked Cassandra. "I don't understand why he can't at least call."

"Sweetheart, he's undercover. That means that no one knows who he really is. He's going by a different name and different identity. If he calls to talk to you and someone inadvertently or deliberately taps into that phone call, it could endanger his life. And they will find out that he isn't really who they think he is."

"Skip didn't tell me all that."

"He probably didn't want you to worry. Now, take your concerns to the Lord, and go pray for him."

"Mom, you don't even believe in God."

"Maybe not, but you do. So does Skip."

Shawn crossed the street and strolled to the park, one hand in his pocket. The more he exercised his leg, the less his muscles ached. His legs had bruises that he couldn't explain, but that didn't slow him down. A warm breeze ruffled his hair as he walked, watching children play and mothers stroll their babies.

With a sorrowful sigh, he shuffled to the duck pond. A father handed his young sons duck feed to toss onto the water. Shawn bit his lower lip to keep it from trembling. Scooping up a small stone, he tossed it into the water.

I wonder where I belong.

A patrol car pulled up to the curb and a police officer started toward him.

Shawn gasped. *I knew it. Mr. Masterson did send the police after me.* Spinning around, he bolted, and the officer dashed after him.

His heart thumped so hard, he thought it would pop out of his chest. He crossed the park in seconds, nearly losing the patrolman in pursuit, and he reached the sidewalk just as two more cruisers rounded the corner.

He had to get away. He wasn't going to jail for any reason.

Changing direction, he fled down the sidewalk and crossed the street. Now there were four police officers chasing him.

Shawn raced around the corner and ducked into a hotel lobby. He stumbled to a stop at the large and beautiful interior. Two separate wide spiral staircases on opposite sides of the lobby led to the second and third floor rooms, while a set of elevators were strategically positioned between them.

Glancing around the lobby for a good place to duck out of sight, Shawn hustled toward a nearby corridor. He didn't know where it would take him, but he didn't care. He just wanted to hide until the police abandoned their search for him.

The four police officers reached the corner and stopped. They looked every direction, but the boy had disappeared.

"Boy, can that kid run." Officer William Jillyan rested his hands on his knees and leaned down to catch his breath. "He's athletic. When we finally catch him, we'd better be prepared for a struggle."

Too winded to talk, the other officers nodded in agreement.

"He's ... he's ... he's got to be here s-s-somewhere," gasped Officer Aaron Menetti. "Maybe he went into this hotel. He disappeared so fast, he had to go into one of these buildings."

"We'll split up," said William. "If necessary, we'll search them all."

The officers separated, each going into a different establishment. William entered the hotel lobby and glanced around. The hotel was so spread out, he knew he couldn't complete a thorough search by himself, so he questioned those in the lobby, but no one had seen a boy matching Shawn's description.

Having questioned a number of people, he concluded that Shawn likely hadn't entered the hotel, but he decided to browse the upper floors anyway. Too tired to take the stairs, the officer trudged over to the elevator. The elevator doors swished open and a middle aged man in swimming attire stepped out with a blue and white striped towel around his neck.

"Good afternoon, Officer. You look exhausted."

"I am. I just ran about ten blocks."

"Chasing someone?"

"As a matter of fact, yes."

"What did he look like? Maybe I've seen him."

"Blond hair, dark glasses, plaid shirt ..."

"Is he dangerous?"

"No, he's not dangerous. Just scared." William stepped into the elevator and rode up to the next floor.

With the adrenaline-rush of the pursuit behind him, after that heart-pounding, ten-block chase, Shawn's leg throbbed and he desperately needed respite.

Strolling down the corridor looking for a place to hide, he came across a door labeled "Men's Locker Room." Pushing open the door, Shawn cautiously stepped inside.

He grinned. *Boy, no one will find me in here.*

Strolling through the locker room, he realized that the door on the opposite side of the room led to the indoor swimming pool. And there are always chairs in a pool area. That would be a great place to sit down and rest for a minute.

William strolled through the second floor but all he saw were closed doors and various staircases. Unless that boy managed to slip into someone's room, he wasn't on the second floor. Now there were emergency exits in several locations, and Shawn could be hiding in one of them. But it appeared that all the activity was on the first level.

Keying his mic, he radioed the other officers. After searching the surrounding buildings, they all came to one conclusion. Shawn had to be in the hotel somewhere.

Sitting off by himself at a small, round table, Shawn watched the kids play in the pool. He felt so isolated and alone. Did he have family? Did anyone at all care about him?

A preteen boy pulled out another chair and plopped down beside him. Startled, Shawn jumped to his feet

"Sorry," said the boy. "I didn't mean to startle you. But my dad said he thought you might need a friend. So he told me to stay with you for awhile."

"Oh? And who's your dad?"

The youth pointed toward a man with a blue and white towel around his neck.

Shawn cocked his head as he watched the man enter the Men's Locker Room.

"Um, thanks, but I think I'd better be going."

"Why?" asked the boy. "Are you in a hurry to get somewhere?"

"No."

"What's your name?"

"Shawn. What's yours?"

116

"Jimmy. We're on vacation here in Laramie. We live in Montana. Where are you from?"

Shawn grimaced and looked away.

"You're lost, aren't you?" said Jimmy. "I can tell by that look on your face."

"I'm not really lost. I'm actually confused. I just need a quiet place to sit where no one will bother me so I can think and regroup and decide my best course of action."

"Oh, I know a great place. Come with me."

Meeting the other officers in the lobby downstairs, William posted an officer at every exit and entrance.

Jimmy's dad hustled over to him. "The boy you're looking for is in the pool area." He pointed toward the glass enclosure that surrounded the indoor swimming pool. "You can get in there through the men's locker room, which is down that hallway."

"Thanks," said William.

Several officers headed for the men's locker room, but when they poured into the pool area, there was no sign of Shawn.

"He's in this building somewhere," said William. "Let's spread out and find him. With half the department here, we have enough officers to cover every square foot of this place."

Shawn followed Jimmy up a back staircase to a room on the third floor. Jimmy used his room key to unlock the door, and they entered the room.

"No one will bother you up here," said Jimmy. "My family will be down by the pool for hours." Jimmy pulled a bottle of water from the cooler and handed it to Shawn.

"Thanks, I am so thirsty." Popping the lid, he downed the water in no time.

"So have you had enough time to think and regroup and come up with your best course of action?" asked Jimmy.

Shawn shook his head. "No. And this isn't a good place to do it. If your dad asked you to stay with me for awhile and then left the pool area, he must know that the police are looking for me. And when they see that neither one of us are at the pool, they'll come looking for me. And this is the first place they'll look."

With a weary sigh, he pulled open the door and stepped into the hallway.

Jimmy ran after him. "Why are the police looking for you?"

"For beating up some guys. But it was self defense."

"How many were there?"

"Three."

"You beat them up all by yourself? Wow!" Jimmy followed him down the hallway.

Chapter 16

Filled with Confusion

With his officers scattered all over the hotel, William stood at the top of one of the spiral staircases, simply surveying the activity below him. Glancing around, he spotted Shawn from a distance strolling down a third-floor hallway, headed toward the stairs.

Keying his mic, he radioed the other officers of Shawn's location.

Just as he reached the stairs, Shawn caught sight of William. Spinning around, he bolted toward the other end of the hallway. Reaching the emergency exit, Jimmy right behind him, he bounded down the stairs two at a time. He would have kept going, but Jimmy grabbed his arm and steered him onto the second floor. Good thing, too, or he would have run right into the two officers who were on their way up.

Halfway down the hallway, Jimmy ducked into a little side corridor and Shawn followed him. Slipping into a dead end crevice, the boys listened intently. If no one saw them enter that little side corridor, they'd be safe for quite awhile.

"Where'd they go? They just disappeared."

Arriving at the hotel with his two daughters, Carl Masterson followed the radio traffic. The police had narrowed their field of search, and William took charge. Shawn was somewhere on the second floor.

The boys listened as the officers ran back and forth down the second-floor hallway. A few minutes later, everything got quiet.

"They gave up," whispered Jimmy, stepping out of hiding.

"Yeah, but where are they?" asked Shawn. He followed Jimmy down the small corridor back to the hallway.

Jimmy glanced both ways before turning left.

The boys crept down the corridor and weren't met by anyone coming from either direction.

Just as they reached the spiral staircase, a couple of police officers on the ground floor looked up and spotted them. The mere sight of their uniforms filled Shawn with fear.

Spinning around, they raced down the hallway to the emergency exit. Hearing voices from below them, and with two officers coming up from behind them, Shawn reached the emergency exit and scampered up to the third floor, Jimmy right behind him.

Shawn and Jimmy raced down the hallway toward the spiral staircase. Seeing two uniformed officers plodding up the staircase toward them, Shawn jerked to a stop. He glanced behind him and saw two other officers closing the gap as they strolled toward him.

None of them were approaching fast, but he now had no place to run.

"The elevators," whispered Jimmy.

Reaching the top of the spiral staircase, the boys dashed down the hallway to the elevators and punched the button. Shawn anxiously waited for the elevator car to reach them while police officers slowly approached them from both directions.

The doors swished open, and Shawn felt lightheaded at the sight of more uniformed officers.

"Let's go, son." Approaching him from either side, the officers gently directed him into the elevator.

Leaving Jimmy standing there, the elevator car carrying Shawn and a half dozen uniformed officers, started its descent to the ground floor.

Fragmented flashbacks of the police surged through his mind, making him wonder how often he'd run from the police in the past. Why else would such visions assault his memory?

Oh, boy. Shawn slid down to the floor in the corner, surrounded by uniformed police officers. When the elevator doors opened up on the lobby level, everyone in the hotel lobby had gathered to see the cause of a thorough police search. Four officers exited the elevator. Shawn glanced up at the two patrolmen standing on either side of him.

"Come on, son, let's go."

Breathing heavily, two police officers lifted him to his feet and marched him from the elevator, through the lobby, and outside to Carl Masterson.

"Here he is, sir."

Carl laughed at all the worn-out patrolmen. "I can't believe that one boy could exhaust the entire Laramie Police Department." Turning to Shawn, his expression sobered.

Shawn's eyes bounced from the girls to their dad. On either side of him, the police officers maintained firm grips on his arms. He tensed, waiting for a word from Carl – a word that would throw him in jail. He had no idea what had happened to him, what brought him here, or how to escape.

Last night, Carl Masterson intended to turn him over to the police and press charges against him simply for being in the house. Yet, he apparently sent the police after him for leaving.

Shawn's intense gaze made Carl smile. "Shawn, why did you take off?"

I don't belong there. You don't want me there. I'm surprised you wasted your time coming after me.

"What happened between you and Michael?" Cupping Shawn's chin, Carl turned his head. A soft whistle escaped his lips. "He gave you quite a shiner."

With all eyes on Shawn, silence settled over everyone. Worming her way between him and the officer on his right, Billie cuddled up to him, looping her arm through his. "Hey, Shawney, talk to Dad. The truth is always important to him."

Shawn glanced from Billie back to Carl. He suspected that was true, but he didn't know why.

Carl knew he had to handle this situation very delicately. He was open to a serious lawsuit that could destroy everything he'd worked for his entire life. His family. His business. His reputation. His good name. *Everything!*

It was imperative he convince Shawn to return home with them, which meant that boy had to feel respected and cared for at all cost. It was obvious that his daughters genuinely cared about him.

And Martha really likes him. So it's up to me to show him the same loving care my family has already shown him.

"Shawn, tell me what happened," said Carl.

With pursed lips, Shawn's eyes drifted over the sea of concerned faces. Last night, anger and hostility surrounded him. This morning, the atmosphere of the people permeated the air with a caring spirit, yet they held him against his will.

Feeling jostled to his left, Shawn noticed that Jayme had crowded between him and the police officer.

"Shawn?" Carl's voice was soft, but persistent.

Fearful that he would accidentally say the wrong thing, he remained silent.

Carl heaved a frustrated sigh and looked away.

Shawn grimaced in anticipation of another explosive outburst.

"Dad, may I suggest that you give him some space," said Billie. "He's frightened."

Carl nodded toward William.

At William's gesture, the police officers widened their circle. However, the Masterson girls snuggled close to him, their arms looped through his, keeping him still. It was clear to him that they weren't going to release him until he explained his actions.

Shawn drew in a slow, deep breath. "I left because I don't belong there. I apologize for hurting your servants. Michael forced me into a fistfight, and when two of your men grabbed me, I took them all down."

"Yes. I saw the results of your handiwork. When we left, Michael was still holding his stomach and my servants could hardly walk. Are you all right?"

Shawn raised an eyebrow. "Why are you concerned about me? I'm just a problem."

"Why do you say that?"

"You said to Michael, 'He's not your problem.' Well, I don't intend to be anybody's problem."

"I'm sorry, Shawn. I didn't mean it like that. Bad choice of words. I consider you my responsibility right now."

"Why? Last night you wanted to press charges against me."

"Last night I didn't have all the facts."

"What are the facts? I have no idea what's going on."

"Come, and I'll tell you." Carl motioned for Shawn to follow him. "We'd like you to return home with us. Michael won't bother you again. You have my word."

"Come on, Shawn." Billie guided him toward the car. "We'll tell you all about it over lunch."

Carl opened the front seat passenger's door and motioned for him to get in.

Shawn paused. He glanced at Carl, then over at the open door. Bits of memories surfaced as he recalled opening the door for someone else, but he couldn't remember who.

"Let's go, Shawn. Jump in." Carl waited patiently by the open car door. Having released their hold on him, Billie and JJ now stood behind him, along with a dozen police officers who semi-surrounded him and the car. They were all awaiting his decision.

Shawn looked at Carl. "No! I don't belong there. I apologize for intruding."

Chapter 17

The Bottom Line

Shawn spun around and collided with the girls. Trying to regain his footing without knocking them down, he lost his balance and tumbled to the sidewalk. If he weren't banged and bruised enough, he just added concrete abrasions to his hands and arms.

Jayme and Billie dropped to his side.

"Shawn, are you OK?" Billie grasped his hand and helped him to his feet. With a firm grip on his hand, she gazed into his eyes through his dark glasses. "We're sorry for getting you into this mess."

Jayme rested her hand on top of Shawn's and Billie's. "Yeah, this is our fault. Thanks for everything you did for us."

Tears filled Billie's eyes. Releasing his hand, she embraced him and kissed his cheek.

Shawn raised an eyebrow. "Thanks for everything I did for you? What did I do for you?"

Billie smiled. "Come with us, and we'll tell you about it over lunch. You have questions. We can see the confusion in your eyes."

Was it that obvious? Shawn's stomach growled, and his gaze shifted from Jayme to Carl. His desire to know what had happened to him swayed his decision.

"I'd really like to know what happened, but I'll have to pass on lunch."

"You're not hungry?" asked Carl.

"I have no money."

"Hm. I guess that could be a problem if I didn't already owe you for bringing my daughters home last night. Let's see, I owe you gas money, money for your time, wear and tear on your vehicle ..."

"A new vehicle," added Jayme.

Billie nodded her assent.

With a raised eyebrow, Carl shot a glance at his daughters.

"You should see his car after Crystal ran into it. She just about totaled it."

"I thought she ran into him."

"Oh, she did." Billie lowered her voice. "Moments before she smashed head-on into his car."

He was hit by a car? That explained some of his bruises. Now he *had* to hear the rest of the story.

Shawn glanced around at the others, but no one else appeared to be close enough to hear Billie's comment.

"Come on, son. Let's go get lunch." Still standing by the open, front passenger's door, Carl gestured for him to get in. Billie crawled into the back seat.

"All right, but I reserve the right to make the decision whether I stay with you or choose to leave."

"Fair enough," said Carl.

With that settled, Shawn slid into the back seat beside Billie, and Jayme scrambled in after him, sandwiching him in the middle.

Carl shrugged and closed the front door. He hustled around to the driver's side and drove them to a fancy restaurant.

Once inside, he seated Shawn and the girls before excusing himself.

"Where's he going?" asked Shawn.

"He's going to call Devon and tell him not to hold lunch for us," said Jayme.

"Shawn, we can tell you what happened while we're waiting for Dad," said Billie.

The girls expounded on the events of the night before, elaborating on the ways he'd come to their aid. Returning to the table, Carl couldn't hide his surprise at what he heard.

"We're sorry, Shawn. We never meant for any of this to happen," said Jayme. "But now you know why Dad considers you his responsibility."

Shawn stared down at his folded hands. "That also explains his reaction to me last night."

"And his sudden change toward you this morning," added Billie. "That's also why, when you ran off this morning, he dropped everything to come look for you. Shawn, please don't go. If you leave before you regain your memory and something bad happens to you, we'll never forgive ourselves. Please stay with us. Dad's trying to locate your family."

"So what if he finds them? They'd be strangers to me. I don't want to stay, but I feel like I can't leave. I'm trapped."

"Shawn, may I offer a suggestion?" asked Carl.

"Please do."

"First off, there's no rush for you to decide. From what I understand, your car was crunched pretty good. Let's get it into the body shop and see if it's salvageable. If we can get it repaired in a timely manner, you'll have wheels."

"That makes sense."

"That will also give you time to regain your memory, and we may locate your family during that time."

Shawn pondered his options. He didn't like Michael, and he feared Carl's anger. He'd gotten a taste of the man's hot temper last night. Now he wondered how easily Carl exploded and if he might inadvertently light the man's fuse. If he opted to leave a second time, would Carl hold him against his will? He obviously had the backing of the entire police department. Was his freedom more important than a hot meal and a comfortable bed? *Yes.*

"Thank you, sir, but I'll hit the road from here."

"Not from here," said Carl. "All your things are at my house. You had sixty five dollars in your wallet. You'll need it."

"I had money on me? What did you do with it?"

"I put it in the safe. Now let's run home to pick up your things, and I'll put you up in a motel for as long as you need."

"You'd do that for me?"

"You need someplace to stay until you're reunited with your family. I'd prefer you to stay with us, but if you won't, I'll assist you financially in any way I can."

Shawn studied him. He didn't want to be a bother to anyone, but this man was going out of his way to assist him. Should he refuse Carl's help altogether or accept his offer to stay with his family temporarily?

"Mr. Masterson, why was I under constant surveillance by a guard?"

"For several reasons. I don't know you and thought it unwise to allow you unsupervised access to my manor. The house is so large, you could get lost again. I wanted someone with you if Michael started something. And due to your physical condition, I didn't want you alone. As long as you're under my roof, you'll be guarded. It's for your own protection."

"And if I decide to leave later?"

"Please be courteous and let me know. I shall not hold you against your will or send the police after you again."

Carl may have a bad temper, but something told Shawn that he was a man of his word. "OK. I'll stay."

Carl breathed a sigh of relief. This situation was a lawsuit ready to explode in his face. That's all he needed. Keeping Shawn with them sheltered him from inquisitive reporters and the possibility of his story hitting the papers.

As owner of the creation, design, and manufacturing of some of the hottest-selling children's video games, Carl had an image to maintain. A new game promising to be a best-seller was scheduled for distribution within the week, and his beautiful triplets had participated in the television promotion for the game.

If word got out that one of his daughters had hit someone with *his car* on *his* property, it would be all over the news. He was already open to a serious lawsuit. Parents might boycott his games. His good name and reputation would be shot down like a duck during hunting season.

Chapter 18

Verbal Warfare

When Carl and his daughters returned home with Shawn, Crystal abandoned her walk with Michael, running to the car to welcome him back. Even through his closed car window, Carl heard Michael's yelling.

"Crystal, you get back here this minute!"

"Shawn, are you all right?" Crystal helped him from the car. "I was worried about you."

"You were?"

"Of course. I'm glad you're safe. Come in the house, and we'll get you something to eat."

"Crystal!" hollered Michael.

"Thank you, but I already ate. Michael is calling you."

"No, Michael is yelling at me, and he can yell all he wants. I'm not his property."

"Aren't you engaged?" asked Shawn.

Crystal nodded sorrowfully. "Unfortunately yes, but that makes me his fiancée, not his possession. I wish he could see the difference."

Carl strolled across the yard to talk to his future son-in-law.

Michael glared at him. "Carl, how could you bring him back here after what he did to me? That hoodlum belongs in jail!"

"Michael, what have you got against him? Shawn is not a hoodlum."

"How do you know? You don't even know him."

"That's true. But he's polite, clean cut, well-dressed, and well mannered. Those are not the characteristics of a hoodlum. He told me that you forced him into a fistfight."

"And you believe him, I suppose."

Narrowing his eyes, Carl scrutinized Michael. "At this point, I'm not sure what to believe, but he's the one with a black eye. Not you."

"Yeah. Yeah. It just so happens, I fought back."

"You sure did, while Levi and Grant restrained him, preventing him from defending himself. Only cowards fight *that* way."

Michael angrily looked away. "Crystal likes him, y'know."

"So do I."

"Well, I don't!"

"The feeling's mutual. He doesn't like you, either."

"I forbid Crystal to associate with him in any way."

"Michael, that boy is a guest in our home, and my daughter, who is not yet married and still lives under my roof of protection, is required to abide by my rules, not yours. And right now she enjoys his company as much as the rest of us."

"I don't care! She's promised to me and will soon be mine. I forbid her to speak to another man. Ever!" Michael stormed away.

Good gracious. He's overcome with jealousy. Carl pondered Michael's bitter words, watching him cross the yard and enter the house. Trailing him into the house, Carl inquired of everyone's whereabouts.

"Jayme, Billie, and Shawn are watching television, sir. I assigned Kenny to stay with Shawn."

"Thank you, Devon. What about Crystal and Michael?"

"They're in the kitchen."

Carl stepped into the recreation room and glanced around. Shawn lay on the floor watching a Disney movie, his head propped on his hand, while the girls nestled in plush armchairs. Kenny stood at parade rest just inside the door.

"Kenny, have a seat and enjoy the program." Carl turned, following the sounds of a bitter argument that drifted down the hallway and led him into the kitchen.

"If I catch you near him again, so help me I'll ..."

"You'll what?" demanded Crystal.

"Never mind what I'll do. You'll regret it. That's all!"

"Michael, I like that boy. You hurt him, and I'll never forgive you. Never!"

"You're engaged to me, and I forbid you to talk to anyone else, even that freeloader."

"He's not a freeloader!"

"Yes, he is, and you know it. So stay away from him!"

"I don't have to take orders from you."

"You do if you want to marry me."

"Well, I have news for you, Mr. Big Shot. I *don't* want to marry you."

"Ah-ha!" cried Michael. "You're throwing me for that young punk. Wait until I get my hands on him. He'll regret the day he met you."

"Leave him alone, Michael."

"No, Crystal. *You* leave him alone!" His whole body flushed and trembling, Michael stormed from the kitchen.

Crystal ran past her father and up the stairs.

"Crystie?"

Crystal paused on the stairs and glanced back at him. "Please, Dad, I'd like to be alone for awhile."

Carl watched until she disappeared around the corner at the top of the stairs.

"What was that all about?" asked his wife.

"Michael and Crystal just had a fight."

"Over what?"

"Over Shawn. Michael's jealous of him."

"You're not serious."

Carl nodded. "Haven't you seen it? This behavior started last night, and it's only getting worse."

"Poor Michael. I'll invite him for dinner tonight. That will give him a chance to get to know Shawn."

Martha was such a dreamer. That's why he loved her so much. Without her continual encouragement, he might never have pursued the business idea that made him the success he is today. Yet, how could he tell his wife that nothing would change Michael's behavior? He was a bitter, angry, and jealous young man.

That thought caused Carl to raise an eyebrow. *And I'm forcing Crystal to marry him?*

Chapter 19

Going Under

After the movie, Shawn and the girls played several games of checkers.

"Where's Crystal?" asked Shawn.

Billie jumped his last checker. "That's a good question. Where is Crystal?"

"Not a clue," said Jayme. With their checker tournament complete, she folded the checkerboard and dropped it back in the box. Her sister dumped the checkers onto it and replaced the lid. "Hey, Billie, let's go swimming before supper. Shawn, can you swim?"

"I don't know."

"Well, let's find out," said Billie.

The girls dashed out the door and bounded up the stairs. Setting the checker set on the end table, Shawn ran after them, Kenny right behind him. The girls reached Crystal's closed bedroom door and banged on it.

"Come in," said Crystal.

Billie pushed open the door, and the foursome filed into the room. "Hey, do you want to go ... Crystie, what's the matter? You've been crying."

Her eyes puffy and red, Crystal sat on her bed with cards spread out before her, playing solitaire. "It's an allergy," she said with a sniffle.

"You sure you're all right?" asked Jayme.

"I'm fine." Crystal smiled at Shawn.

"We're taking a dip before supper," said Billie. "You want to join us?"

"Sure."

Shawn glanced at the triplets hesitantly. Jayme's question haunted him. Could he swim?

"Shawn?" Billie's soft voice broke into his thoughts.

"Miss?"

The girls burst into giggles.

"Miss." echoed Crystal. "Shawney, despite amnesia, your upbringing comes through loud and clear. You're always polite and respectful. Now, if you'll excuse me, I need to change. I'll meet you guys down at the pool."

Jayme and Billie darted from the room and dashed opposite directions. Shawn and Kenny followed them into the hallway. Crystal's door closed behind them, and the bedroom doors on either side clicked shut.

Looking back at the closed bedroom doors, Shawn breathed a soft sigh. The girls treated him like their brother. In an unfamiliar setting with no recollection of his past, he treasured their attentiveness and felt lost without them. But did he really want to face the possibility that he might not be able to swim?

Kenny smiled at him. "Come, Shawn. I'll show you back to your room so you can get ready to go swimming, too."

"Um ..." Shawn started to decline the invitation when a door opened.

Still fully dressed, Billie dashed over to him and grabbed his hand. "You're coming with us, aren't you, Shawn?"

Shawn didn't reply. What if he couldn't swim? If one of these girls had to save him from drowning, that would humiliate him.

With a tender smile, Billie squeezed his hand. "I'm sure you're a good swimmer. And after all you've been through, you'll find the warm water soothing and the afternoon sun relaxing."

"I doubt I packed any swimming trunks."

"You did," said Kenny.

"Great. We'll meet you and Kenny at the pool." Billie rushed back to her room and started to close the door. Poking her head out one last time, she said, "Kenny, why don't you change and join us?"

Kenny smiled. "Another time, Li'l Lady."

Shawn raised an eyebrow and looked at Kenny.

"I know that look, but it's not what you think. I searched your suitcase looking for information – anything to help us locate your family." Leading Shawn to the stairs, Kenny escorted him back to his room.

With a sigh, Shawn trudged over to the suitcase and rummaged through it, locating a pair of trunks. *Rats.*

Kenny stepped into the hallway to give him privacy. Shawn stripped off his clothes, horrified by the massive bruising and abrasions that covered him. Did he not notice how bruised he was when he dressed this morning, or was he more discolored now? He couldn't go outside like this. The dark discoloration contrasted sharply with his fair skin.

"Kenny?"

Kenny stepped into Shawn's room and cringed. "Oh, my."

"I can't go outside looking like this."

"A tee shirt might cover some of the abrasions on your arms."

Shawn slipped on a gleaming white undershirt. "Barely, if at all."

"Don't worry about it, Shawn. Those bruises tell the story of what brought you here in the first place, and the girls are part of that story. So you needn't try to hide your physical condition from them."

Shawn pulled off his tee shirt and tossed it back into the suitcase. "Good. I didn't want to wear a shirt swimming anyway."

"Then let's go. The girls are anxiously awaiting your arrival." Kenny escorted Shawn down to the pool and seated himself in a nearby lawn chair.

"I don't really need a baby-sitter." Shawn strolled to the edge of the deck.

"I know you don't, son. Try to think of me as your own, personal bodyguard."

"Come on, Shawn," called Crystal. "Jump in. The water's great."

Strolling to the edge of the deck, Shawn's eyes skimmed the water of the gigantic pool. Two of the triplets sat on a raft floating in the middle of the deep end, but where was the third? A sudden shove sent him toppling into the water. Shawn surfaced, spitting out water.

Billie giggled triumphantly on the pool deck. "Look, Shawney, you can swim."

The girls laughed. Billie tossed a beach ball into the water and dived over Shawn, swimming out to join her sisters.

"Catch, Shawn." Billie tossed him the ball.

Shawn bopped it back. Abandoning their raft, Jayme and Crystal joined the volleyball game, followed by a swimming competition. After racing him across the pool, the triplets crawled onto the raft. Shawn dove under and tipped them over.

"Hey!" The girls surfaced, spitting water.

"That does it, Shawn. You've had it!" cried Billie.

Shawn laughed. "Got to catch me, first." He swam toward the shallow end, expecting the triplets to chase him.

Watching them play from the third-floor balcony, Martha gasped when one of her daughters floundered in the deep end of the pool and went under. And while the other two raced after Shawn, oblivious to their sister's distress, the girl struggled to reach the surface.

"Oh, my goodness!" Carl bolted toward the door. "Stay here and try to get their attention."

Martha yelled to Kenny and the swimmers, pointing toward the middle of the pool, but they obviously couldn't make out what she was saying since Kenny took no action and her daughters simply waved.

Chapter 20

The Wrong Patient

Shawn reached the pool's edge and hoisted himself out of the water. Spinning around, his gaze shot past the two girls following him and zeroed in on Crystal, who was thrashing about in the water. Skip could easily identify her by the bright pink color of her bathing suit. She struggled to reach the surface for a breath of air.

Sprinting across the pool deck, Shawn dived back into the water, shooting toward her like a missile. He grasped one of her flailing arms, attempting to pull her above the water, but by now she was so panicked that she yanked away from him, spinning him under the water. From behind him, Crystal grabbed his left wrist and shoulder, holding him under water as she tried to climb on top of him.

Carl had never descended three flights of stairs so fast in his entire lifetime. As he flew down the last flight, Devon stood at the front door welcoming Michael into the house.

"Devon, call the rescue squad! One of the girls is drowning!"

"Drowning!" cried Michael. "Which one?"

Rounding the stairs, Carl bolted down the hallway, through the great room, and out the patio door to the large pool area, Michael on his heels. Dodging the patio furniture, the men dashed onto the pool deck.

Carl gasped at the sight of his daughter holding Shawn under water. Kenny had already kicked off his shoes and dived into the pool. His other two daughters furiously swam to their aid. For him or Michael to jump in at this point would be futile. Martha joined them, and the three looked on helplessly. Carl feared that his panicked daughter was about to drown that boy, and he couldn't prevent it.

Fighting panic, Shawn slapped his right hand onto his left shoulder, tightly grasping Crystal's right wrist. Pulling her hand loose, he ducked under his right arm and placed her hand onto his right shoulder. Almost immediately, she released his left wrist and encircled his neck with her left arm. Maintaining a firm grip on her right wrist, Shawn grabbed her left arm to loosen her choke hold around his neck, and he kicked to the surface.

Shawn and Crystal bobbed to the surface gasping for breath. Seeing Kenny and the girls a swim-stroke away, Shawn released her right wrist. Crystal threw her free arm around his neck, clinging to him, breathing hard, and trembling uncontrollably. Kenny and her sisters attempted to free him from her iron grasp.

Hardly able to breathe with Crystal hanging onto him, Shawn struggled to tread water, expending tremendous energy to keep her from dragging him under again.

Sliding his arm around her for support, Kenny attempted to loosen her death grip on Shawn.

"Crystie, let him go," said Jayme

The instant Crystal loosened her hold, Shawn ducked under water and out of her arms. Bobbing up beside her, he grasped her right arm while Kenny supported her on the left. With Crystal safely between them, they swam to the side of the pool.

Carl and Michael reached down and grasped her arms, lifting her out of the water and setting her on the deck. Crystal melted into her mother's arms sobbing.

Martha soothed her. "Shh. You're okay, sweetie, thanks to Shawn. You nearly drowned the poor boy when he tried to rescue you."

Kenny hoisted himself out of the water before grasping Shawn's hand and pulling him from the pool.

Crawling onto the wet deck breathing hard, Shawn sat down to rest. He crossed his arms on his bent knees, rested his head on his arms, and closed his eyes.

Kenny grabbed a towel and dried his dripping clothes. "Mr. Masterson, I'm going to shower and change. I'll meet Shawn at his room, if that's okay."

"That's fine."

Taking slow, deep breaths, Shawn listened to the Masterson family chattering excitedly.

"I thought we'd lost you," said Carl. "And we would have if ... if ..."

"... Shawn hadn't been here," finished Martha.

"Kenny would have saved her," said Jayme.

Carl cleared his throat. "Kenny would have been busy elsewhere. He was only here to guard Shawn."

Billie gasped. "Oh, my gosh! That's right. Jayme and I would have had to save her."

"Would you have been able to? She nearly drowned Shawn in her state of panic. She might have drowned you."

"Kind of ironic, isn't it?" said Billie. "Crystal hits Shawn with the car, and he rescues her from drowning."

"Crystal, are you OK?" Michael's voice carried genuine concern.

"Shawn?" Two soft hands rested on his crossed arms on either side of his head.

Shawn looked into Crystal's eyes as she knelt in front of him.

"Thank you for saving my life." Quick as lightening, she cupped his face in her hands and planted a firm kiss on his cheek.

Shawn jumped at her unexpected expression of gratitude. Michael glared at him, spun on his heel, and stormed into the house. Shawn watched him stomp off before shifting his gaze from the girls to their parents.

"Are you all right?" Billie squatted beside him and touched his arm.

With a faint nod, he rested his head on his arms once again.

"Well, supper is almost ready," said Martha. "I'd like you four to shower and change. Devon, cancel the ambulance."

"Too late," said Carl.

Shawn caught the tension in his voice and looked up. Devon escorted two paramedics through the gate hauling their equipment on a gurney. The names on their uniforms read Craig and Dyllon.

Carl cringed when they headed straight for Shawn. *Great. If they start asking questions ...*

"Let's take a look at you, son," said Craig.

Shawn looked up at them, and the girls moved aside, allowing the paramedics access to him.

"I'm fine, sir. You might want to examine Crystal. She almost drowned."

"We will, but first we want to examine you." Craig cupped his chin to examine his black eye and the big bruise on the side of his head. His partner studied the abrasions on his arms and looked at the bruises on his legs. "What happened? You didn't get these bruises from nearly drowning."

Carl winced, fearful that Shawn would blurt out everything they told him at lunch. Shawn glanced up at him. *Shawn, keep quiet. Please. If you tell them that my daughter hit you with the car, my reputation is shot.*

Craig snapped his fingers in front of Shawn's eyes and redirected his attention. "Don't look at him. Look at me."

Dyllon rose to his feet and addressed the others. "May we go inside and talk?"

Oh, boy, thought Carl. *They want to talk to him privately. They'll ask him leading questions, and there's no telling what he'll say.*

Carl led the way into the house, glancing back at Shawn. Craig squatted beside him, talking softly.

Chapter 21

A Little Family Friction

"Son, what's your name?"

Shawn watched the others enter the house. Now that he was out of the water and sitting still, he felt chilled. A cool breeze made him shiver. "I don't know. I guess it's Shawn."

"You guess?"

"That's what everyone calls me."

"Shawn what? What's your last name?"

"Uh ..." Shawn thought for a moment. "I don't remember."

Craig raised an eyebrow. "You don't remember your last name?"

"No, sir."

"Where do you live?"

"I don't know." Shawn rubbed his arms, wanting to go inside to shower and change.

"You don't know your name, and you don't remember where you live."

Shawn frowned at Craig's condescending tone of voice.

"How did you get a black eye? Who hit you?" demanded Craig.

Shawn glared at him. He didn't like the way this guy interrogated him. "I got into a fistfight, if it's any business of yours."

"With the man who was just out here? He beat you, didn't he?"

"No, sir. Mr. Masterson has been ..."

"What happened in the pool?"

"His daughter nearly ..."

"How did you get beat up?"

Shawn cocked his head. "Why do you keep interrupting me?"

"Why don't you tell me the truth? Or don't you know it? I'd like to run you to the hospital to be examined by a doctor. You have amnesia and have suffered serious abuse. We'll protect you."

"From what?"

"From the abuser."

"I don't need your protection. I can take care of myself."

The paramedic motioned to his physical condition. "Obviously, you can't."

Shawn stood and started toward the house. "This interrogation is over."

Craig grasped his arm and steered him toward the open back gate. "You're going to the hospital to be examined by a doctor."

"No, I'm not." Shaking Craig off his arm, Shawn headed toward the patio door. Before Craig could stop him, Shawn slid open the patio door and entered the house. His eyes bounced from Dyllon to Carl.

Carl glanced at his wife and over at Shawn. Worry creased his brow.

"Mr. Masterson, I don't want to go to the hospital."

"You don't have to go."

"Good." Shawn dodged behind him for protection. One thing he'd learned since he'd been there. *No one* dared cross Carl Masterson. "I'm not going."

With a smile, Carl turned to the paramedics. "You heard him."

Dyllon opened his clipboard and handed it to Carl.

"Sign here as Shawn's guardian, refusing medical treatment for him."

"Oh, I'm not his guardian," said Carl. "He's of legal age. He can sign for himself."

Craig raised an eyebrow. "You're kidding. I thought he was still a minor. How about Crystal?"

Dyllon shook his head. "She wouldn't let me examine her. She said she was OK." Dyllon handed Carl the clipboard. "Sign here refusing medical treatment for your daughter."

Carl signed and Dyllon flipped to the next page before handing it to Shawn.

"Sign here, son."

Shawn drew close to Carl and lowered his voice. "Sir, what's my full name?"

"Shawn Christopher," whispered Carl.

"How do you spell that?"

Carl spelled out his name and Shawn jotted it on the line.

Taking the clipboard, the paramedics gathered their equipment and left.

Carl motioned for Shawn to follow him, and they trotted up the stairs. "You look cold."

"I am. Do I have time to shower before supper?"

"Absolutely. Now, I'm curious what you told the paramedic."

Shawn repeated the conversation to Carl. Reaching the third floor, they started down the hallway.

"So you didn't tell him that Crystal hit you with the car?"

"No, sir. You didn't want me to say anything, and he gave me no reasons to want to talk to him."

"You're incredibly perceptive. Thanks."

When they entered Shawn's room, they found Kenny, freshly showered, sitting at the desk flipping through a magazine. The moment they walked through the door, Kenny leaped to his feet.

"Mr. Masterson, I apologize for inconveniencing you. Had I known that you were bringing him up yourself, I would have come down to get him."

Carl brushed his hand through the air. "Not a problem. I needed to talk to him anyway. Shawn, hurry and shower. Supper is probably ready."

"Yes, sir."

Shawn grabbed clean clothes from his suitcase and hurried into his private bathroom, shutting the door. Through the closed door he overheard Carl talking to Kenny about him.

"I really like that boy. He's a good fighter. I still can't believe he took down Grant, Levi, and Michael single-handedly. I'd like to keep him. I might offer him a position as a security officer."

"You promised him that he could leave at any time."

"I'm not talking about holding him against his will, Kenny. He's bright, caring, honest, trustworthy, thoughtful, fun to be around. I have more respect for him than I've ever had for Michael."

"Sir, should I continue to guard him?"

"Yes, the house is so large, he could easily get lost. And I'm a little concerned about his physical condition. I think it's wise for someone to stay with him at all times."

Shawn turned on the water, adjusting the temperature. He wondered about Carl as he stepped into the steamy shower. Already late for dinner, he took a quick, five-minute shower, dried and dressed himself in pleated, shiny-black slacks and a bright white tee shirt.

His mind lingered on the picture he'd found in his suitcase of a beautiful teenage girl with long, auburn hair. There was no name on the picture and he wondered about her. Was she his sister or cousin? His girlfriend? Just a friend?

Shawn cleaned his glasses and combed his hair before exiting the steamy bathroom. He pulled on black dress socks and black leather walking shoes, quickly tying them. Snatching up a pressed, white dress shirt, he slipped it on and followed Kenny out the door, buttoning it up and tucking it in during their three-flight hike down the stairs.

The moment they entered the dining room, Michael snapped, "Well, it's about time you got here. You've kept us waiting for twenty minutes!"

"Seven, but under the circumstances his tardiness is excusable. Don't you think?" Carl said to Michael.

"Yeah. He could have let Crystal drown, and then he wouldn't have been late," said Billie.

"Shut up!" barked Michael.

Billie and Jayme glanced over at their sister with empathy. It appeared that Michael wasn't nice to anyone.

"Sorry I'm late." Shawn suspected that by now everything about him was under Carl's scrutiny. He slid into the closest available chair, strategically located between Billie and Jayme. The girls, no doubt, saved it for him.

Carl smiled at Shawn when he joined them. One glance around the table explained his smile. Carl wore a nice shirt and slacks like Shawn's. All the ladies wore colorful dresses. Only Michael seemed out of place wearing blue jeans and a denim shirt.

During the evening meal, the tension around the table grew so heavy, even Shawn felt it.

"So how was it?" demanded Michael.

"How was what?" Shawn took a bite of steak.

"You kissed Crystal."

"No, I didn't."

"Michael," whispered Crystal. "You're embarrassing me."

"You should be embarrassed, kissing that freeloading bum like he's a hero or something. You don't kiss me like that."

"You don't deserve a kiss like that."

"Ooo," chorused Jayme and Billie.

Shawn followed the conversation while he ate.

Martha tried to change the subject. "How's the steak?"

"Fabulous!" said Shawn.

The triplets nodded in agreement.

"It needs salt," growled Michael. "And I don't like it with onions. How many times must I tell the cook not to put onions on mine?"

"Then scrape them off," said Shawn. "It's not that much trouble."

Michael glared at him. "Shut up and mind your own business."

"Leave him alone, Michael," cried Billie. "He's our guest."

"He's a freeloader," snapped Michael.

Shawn glanced at him and looked away.

"That's enough, Michael," said Martha. "Shawn is a nice boy, and I will not permit you to talk about him like

157

that. He is a guest in this home, whether or not you like it. If you can't accept that, you may leave."

Silence settled over the dining room. Michael shifted his gaze from person to person, avoiding eye contact with Shawn.

"Yes, of course. I, um, have to go anyway." He rose from his chair and leaned down to give Crystal a quick peck on the cheek, but she pulled away from him. With a sigh, Michael pushed in his chair without the pleasure of the tiniest kiss. "Bye, Crystal. I'll call you later."

Crystal silently nodded.

"Thanks for inviting me, Martha." Michael waved and hurried out the door.

Carl exchanged glances with his wife.

"I'm not hungry, anymore." Crystal pushed her plate aside and left the table in tears.

Shoveling in his last mouthful, Shawn stood and addressed Carl. "That was good, Mr. Masterson. Thank you for inviting me." He quietly pushed in his chair and left the dining room. Kenny followed him.

Jayme and Billie looked at each other, but didn't say anything. Carl and Martha finished eating and went for a walk in the garden.

"That Shawn is a real fine boy," said Carl. "He'd make a great son-in-law."

"And who would you have him marry?"

"Crystal, of course. She's crazy about him, and that Michael does nothing but make her cry. Honestly, Dear, I had no idea he was so jealous."

"Forget it, Carl. The girls love Shawn like a brother, nothing more. Besides that, we don't know his financial status."

"That's true, but he dresses nicely. He's polite and well mannered. He's had a good upbringing. I'll bet he's fairly well off."

"Carl, aren't you forgetting one small detail?"

"What's that?"

"Shawn should have a say in this decision. Don't you think?"

Chapter 22

The Truth Comes Out

Thrusting his hands deep in his pockets, Shawn trudged up to his room, stopping outside the door.

"Kenny, will you give me a tour of the house?"

"Sure, but it's quite a hike. You want to go now?"

"I do. Mr. Masterson won't object. Will he?"

"Not at all. He told me to stay with you. He didn't say to limit your access."

Kenny guided Shawn through the house. They traipsed up and down the stairs, visiting all four floors. They entered rooms through one doorway and left through another. Kenny showed him how to get to the back door and three other exits that made it convenient for everyone coming and going.

"Where are the girls' rooms?"

"Second floor. We're coming up to them now."

The sound of crying reached his ears, and Shawn paused, attempting to pinpoint its location. The sobbing drifted from a nearby bedroom, so he tapped on the closed door.

"Who is it?"

"It's Shawn. Are you OK?"

The door slowly opened. Crystal dried her eyes and motioned for them to enter. She looked miserable.

Shawn and Kenny stepped into her room.

"You want to talk about it?" asked Shawn.

Exploding into tears, she flung herself into his arms, sobbing uncontrollably.

Kenny raised an eyebrow and retreated into the hallway.

Shawn comforted Crystal, letting her cry, and guided her across the room to her bed. Crystal sat down and choked back a sob.

Not wanting to be accused again, Shawn remained standing, taking a step backwards to increase their distance.

"Crystal, am I coming between you and Michael?"

"No, you have nothing to do with it."

"Are you sure? Because I can leave. I'll pack up and be gone first thing in the morning."

"No, Shawn, please don't leave. We enjoy having you here. Besides, Dad will locate your family, and you'll be gone soon enough."

"Then if I'm not the trouble – what is?"

Crystal wrung her hands in her lap and stared out the window.

"Crystal?"

"I don't want to marry Michael."

Shawn cocked his head. "Then why are you?"

"Mom and Dad insist I marry him because he's wealthy. And he says he loves me."

"Do you love him?"

Crystal sighed and shook her head. "I can't stand to be around him. We fight and argue all the time."

"I'm sorry."

"Shawn, you are so pleasant to be around. You're the complete opposite of Michael. Michael is angered so easily, and I never know what will trigger it."

"Have you talked to your parents?"

Crystal nodded. "I tried. They won't listen to me. Michael's wealthy. That's all they care about."

"And what do you care about?"

"Huh? I don't follow you."

"Crystal, I know it's important to honor and obey your parents, but who has to live with him after you're married?"

"Well, I do."

"Then you should have a say in this decision."

"But my parents will leave me out of their will."

"Is it more important that you're wealthy or happy? Think about it." Shawn started toward the door, but Crystal bounced off the bed and grasped his wrist.

"Come with me to talk to them, Shawn. Please."

"You don't need me." Shawn twisted his wrist free.

Crystal bit back more tears. "I'm sorry. That would put you in an awkward position. Wouldn't it?"

Shawn sighed, glancing from Kenny to Crystal. "Come on. I'll go with you."

Sitting at his desk talking on the telephone, Carl ignored the knock on his door.

"Can't you just print his picture without doing a big story?" he asked the editor of the local newspaper.

"I could, but there's a story behind that picture. So if you want his photo in the paper, you'll have to talk to my reporter. He'll be over in twenty minutes."

Carl sighed. "Will it make the morning edition?"

"Sure will."

"OK. Send him over." Carl hung up the phone.

The door rattled again, and he jumped. "What is it?"

Crystal pushed open Carl's office door and poked her head in. "Dad, do you have a minute?"

"Of course, darling." Carl motioned for her to enter. "I always have time for you." He raised an eyebrow when Shawn and Kenny trailed her into his office. "I see you brought reinforcements."

Taking Shawn's hand, she blushed. "Moral support."

Carl nodded toward Kenny. "Leave Shawn here with me, and be back in thirty minutes."

"Yes, sir." Kenny left.

"Now, what did you two want to talk about?"

"Um ..." Crystal looked at Shawn, but he motioned for her to talk. "I ..."

"Tell him, Crystal. Tell your dad like you told me."

Crystal drew in a deep breath and let it out slowly. "I'm sorry Dad, I can't marry Michael. I won't marry Michael. I'm calling off our engagement."

Carl grinned at her announcement.

"You don't object?"

"Not at all. I'm happy for you."

"Thank you, Daddy." Crystal embraced him. Releasing him, she flung her arms around Shawn, nearly knocking him over, and planted a solid kiss on his smooth cheek. "You're the greatest."

Shawn winced.

Amused by his reaction, Carl noted that his daughter's affection had caught him off guard both times.

"Thanks, Dad." Crystal blew her father a kiss and dashed out the door.

"Did you want to see me, sir?" asked Shawn.

"Yes, son. Have a seat." Dropping behind his desk, Carl ignored him while organizing paperwork needing filed.

Shawn slowly sat on the hard-back chair beside Carl's desk.

A few minutes later Devon escorted the reporter into Carl's office. Immediately, he pointed his camera at Shawn, who smiled for his picture.

Pulling up a chair in front of Shawn, the reporter pulled out his notebook and a pen. "I should be using a tape recorder," he said, "but I tend to be a little old fashioned. Besides, from what I've been told, you likely won't be able to answer any of my questions anyway, so why lug around a tape recorder when a pen and note pad is much easier"

Shawn raised an eyebrow at the reporter's speech. He knew what was about to happen. And since he'd woken up in this house with no recollection of his past, it bothered him tremendously that he couldn't answer *anybody's* questions. Maybe this evening, he'd embellish – just a little – and have some fun.

The reporter grasped Shawn's hand in a firm handshake. "My name is Brian. I came to interview you for the *Laramie Boomerang*. So tell me a little something about yourself."

Shawn cocked his head and grinned. His imagination was about to take off on an adventure. After all ... *"I don't know"* was just too mundane. "Like what?" he asked Brian.

"Oh, anything at all. Your hobbies. What you'd like to do with your life. What brought you to Laramie. Your family background."

"Well ..." Shawn paused like he was thinking. "I'm the youngest of twelve boys. My dad was a fighter pilot in the Air Force, and my mom, bless her heart, flew a helicopter."

Carl's mouth dropped open and Brian was scribbling furiously.

"My eleven older brothers all enlisted one by one as they got old enough. But I didn't want to enlist. I always wanted to be a missionary. Only problem was, they all set a precedent and expected me to enlist in the military, preferably the Air Force. Now I like the Air Force best of all branches of the military, but I had my heart set on being a missionary, so I ran away from home. And you know what happened?"

"What?" exclaimed Brian and Carl at the same time.

"They all followed me into the ministry!" Skip burst into laughter.

Carl started laughing. "Shawn, you had me going there for a minute."

But Brian exploded on him. "You're making a mockery of me!"

"No, I'm not," said Shawn, still laughing. "I just thought it was a lot more interesting and definitely more fun than telling you over and over again that I don't know and I can't remember, which I can't. Brian, have you ever had amnesia?"

"No."

"Well, it's horrible not being able to remember things as simple as your name, age, and address."

"I can only imagine how difficult it must be," said Brian. "I hope this article helps you reconnect with your family."

"OK, son, you may go," said Carl. "Kenny should be waiting for you in the hallway."

Shawn quietly left and closed the door.

The reporter whistled softly. "He's definitely got amnesia. What happened?"

"My daughters got stranded with a flat tire, and Shawn brought them home. From what I understand, he took a serious tumble in the driveway and cracked his head."

"Then you don't know him."

"Now, why do you think I called the newspaper?"

"Good point." The reporter folded his small notepad and slipped it into his hip pocket. "Thanks for the information, Mr. Masterson. By the way, how has his stay affected your family?"

"Big time. His presence has brought harmony like we haven't seen in a long time, except for Crystal and Michael, but that problem has been rectified."

"Oh, really? How?"

"Crystal called off her engagement with Michael. Between you and me, I think she's sweet on Shawn. She kissed him twice today. He'd make a fine son-in-law."

Chapter 23

The
Newspaper's Announcement

Shawn trudged up the stairs to the third floor and down the hallway, pushing open his bedroom door.

"Goodnight, Kenny."

Although he no longer needed an escort to find his way up to his room, he knew that Kenny was under orders to stay with him.

"Goodnight, Shawn."

Shawn closed the door. Rummaging through his suitcase, he pulled out pajamas and caught sight of a black, leather Bible. He picked it up and turned it over in his hands. Engraved on the front cover was the name *Skip Shaughnessy.*

That's not my name. Is it?

Shawn set the Bible on the bed and unbuttoned his shirt.

It was in my suitcase. If this is, in fact, my suitcase. But if this book's not mine, then who does it belong to?

Dropping his shirt onto the bed, he yanked on his pajama shirt and buttoned it up.

That's a dumb question. It belongs to Skip Shaughnessy. That's got to be me. Shawn pursed his lips in thought. *And Billie called me Skip until her dad made her stop.*

Shawn kicked off his shoes and dropped his trousers.

But that can't be my name. My driver's license says my name is Shawn Christopher.

He pulled on pajama bottoms and laid his clothes on the foot of the bed before retrieving a toothbrush and toothpaste from his suitcase.

Then who is Skip Shaughnessy, and how did his Bible get into my suitcase?

Shawn brushed his teeth and returned to his room where he snatched up the Bible and crawled into bed. He read for nearly an hour, finding comfort and strength in the words of that black book, yet not knowing why.

Too tired to read any more, Shawn laid the Bible on the nightstand. *I like that book. I think I'll read some more tomorrow.*

He'd had an exhausting day. Flipping off the lamp switch, he lay down on the bed, his fingers interlaced beneath his head as he contemplated the day's events.

First thing in the morning, he'd landed in a fist fight with Michael.

He took off on Mr. Masterson and ended up running from the police.

Crystal almost drowned, and she nearly drowned him in his attempt to rescue her.

Fighting. Running. Swimming. Rescuing. No wonder he was so exhausted.

I shouldn't be here. I have a strange feeling I'm needed somewhere. But where? My name's not Shawn, I don't think. But that's what my driver's license said.

As his eyes dropped shut, his mind whisked him to a familiar place. Everything was a blur as he opened the front door and entered a house. "Skip!" The children's voices bounced off the walls of his mind.

Shawn bolted upright, glancing around the dark room. Everything was still. He lay back down and drifted off to sleep.

Crystal dreaded the thought of talking to Michael, but with her parents' support, she could finally discontinue that nightmarish relationship. And by ending it over the phone, she held the option of disconnecting at any time.

Pacing her bedroom floor, her cordless phone to her ear, Crystal counted the rings. Halfway through the seventh ring, an irritated male voice barked into the phone.

"What do you want?"

Drawing in a lungful of air, Crystal stopped pacing and spit out her announcement in one quick breath. "We're through, Michael. I'm calling off our engagement."

"You're what?"

"You heard me."

"Have you discussed this with your parents? There's somebody else, isn't there? It must be that freeloader who's staying at your house."

"Shawn is not a freeloader!"

"He influenced you, didn't he?"

A thousand answers flooded Crystal's mind, but none that expressed her exact feelings.

"Well, *didn't he?*"

"Yes! He gave me the courage to stand up to you! And that's something I've wanted to do for a long time. I have nothing else to say to you. Goodbye!" Crystal disconnected the call and dropped the phone onto her bed. Crossing her arms, she resumed pacing. "He's absolutely infuriating!"

Expecting Michael to call back to finish their verbal warfare, Crystal darted from her room. Her phone could ring, but she wouldn't hear it.

Billie's open bedroom door was an invitation to anyone walking by, so Crystal popped in. Her sisters sat at the card table in the corner.

"I feel horrible for standing up Tim and Danny the other night," said JJ.

"I do, too," said Billie. "We need to find a way to get out there to see them and give them a proper good-bye."

"Why don't we just ask Dad if we can borrow the car?"

Crystal paced Billie's bedroom floor, wanting to hit something.

"Hey, Crystal, come join us for a game of Go Fish," said Billie.

"I will in a minute. After I calm down."

"Michael again?" asked JJ.

"Isn't it always? But no more! I called off our engagement."

The girls leaped to their feet, practically knocking over their chairs and dashed to Crystal.

"You did what?" exclaimed Billie.

"Does Dad know?" asked JJ.

"How did he take it?" blurted Billie.

"Who? Dad or Michael?"

"Dad, of course," said Billie. "We know how Michael took it."

"Dad's okay with it, believe it or not."

Billie brought her right hand to her forehead and collapsed onto her bed. "No. Are you talking about our dad?"

"That's a miracle in itself," said JJ.

Crystal jerked to a stop. A grin started at one corner of her mouth and spread to the other. "You know, there's something remarkable about Shawn. Since he's come into our home, Dad's calmer than I've ever seen him. Things that used to irritate him, he now takes in stride."

"I've noticed that, too," said Billie. "When you kissed Shawn on the pool deck, I expected Dad to explode into tiny, little pieces."

"I have a confession. I kissed him again in front of Dad in his office, and it didn't faze him in the least."

"How did Shawn react?" said JJ.

Crystal giggled. "Surprised."

"Where is Shawn, anyway?" asked Billie. "Maybe he'd like to play cards with us."

"Let's go ask him," said Jayme.

The triplets trotted up the stairs to the third floor. They found Kenny sitting on a chair outside Shawn's door reading a book.

"Hi, Kenny. Is Shawn in his room?" asked Crystal.

"He went to bed."

"At this hour?" said Billie. "It's not even nine o'clock."

At the sound of Shawn's voice, the foursome jumped and looked at the closed bedroom door.

"Stop, or I'll shoot!"

Kenny and the triplets burst into his room. Shawn thrashed about in his sleep, nearly tumbling off the bed.

"Drop that gun!"

The girls rushed to him.

Billie seized his wrists. "Shawn, wake up. You're dreaming. Shawn!"

He yanked away from her and shoved her off the bed. Almost immediately, he clapped his hands over his ears as if he'd heard a loud noise.

Grasping his arms, Crystal rattled him. "Shawn!"

Awakened with a start, he scrambled into her arms.

Crystal drew him close, soothing him like she would her little brother. "Relax, sweetie, it was just a bad dream."

From out of nowhere, Carl darted into the room. "What's all the commotion in here?" He jerked to a stop when he saw Shawn nestled in Crystal's arms.

"Shawn had a nightmare," said JJ.

"I see."

Shawn tensed, resisting Crystal's sisterly embrace. Not wanting her father to get the wrong impression, Crystal released him.

"A glass of warm milk might help him sleep better," said Carl.

Shawn grimaced.

"On second thought, make that hot chocolate. I suspect he doesn't like warm milk."

Crystal rested her hand on his arm. "Shawn, you want some cocoa?"

Carl smiled at Shawn and left the room.

"Boy, that was some nightmare you had," said Billie.

"Oh, my gosh, it was so real," said Shawn. "Like I was really there, battling some lunatic who was shooting at me."

"What have you been watching on television?" asked JJ. "Maybe those scenes were somewhere in your subconscious due to a program you watched on TV."

"I hope that's all it was."

"You want to play cards with us?" asked Crystal.

"Might as well. I'm wide awake now."

The next morning, Shawn rolled out of bed and dressed by seven thirty. Opening his bedroom door, he stepped into the hallway. "Hi, Kenny, did you stand guard over my door all night?"

"No, I went to bed around eleven and got up a little before seven." Kenny escorted him down the stairs. "You're up early this morning. Since breakfast is served promptly at eight, you'll be on time, and Mr. Masterson will appreciate that."

Reaching the dining room, Shawn and Kenny stopped outside the closed door. They exchanged glances, reluctant to enter and interrupt the argument in progress.

"I said nothing of the kind!" yelled Carl. "I didn't even *hint* that Crystal and Shawn are engaged."

"Well, what *did* you say?" demanded Martha

"That she called off her engagement with Michael."

"That's all?"

"Um, I guess I also told the reporter that she's sweet on Shawn, and I think he'd make a great son-in-law. But I didn't think he'd print it as an upcoming engagement!"

"He printed it, all right. And I'm telling you right now, Carl, there's nothing going on between Shawn and Crystal."

"Of course, there is. She kisses him. She hugs him. She's protective of him."

Shawn tensed. Although Crystal's affections left him uneasy, he considered it a sisterly love, and he felt certain that's how she intended it. Yet Carl believed it to be more.

"Watch them, Carl. She hugs and kisses him like a brother, not a boyfriend. And he hasn't figured out how to respond to her show of affection."

"OK! So I made a mistake!"

"A *big* mistake. I've already received three phone calls from so-called relatives who have claimed him."

Carl groaned. "Oh, no. What did you tell them?"

"What could I tell them? I gave them directions how to get here. You can take it from there."

"OK. Have Devon call the police and send over a squad car. Since Shawn has amnesia, he won't recognize anybody, even if they're genuine. So I'll have to ask for proof, and that's going to make some folks angry. We might need the police. What a shame. He would have made such a fine son-in-law, too."

Chapter 24

Word Travels Fast

Due to the newspaper's proclamation that amnesia victim Shawn Christopher was engaged to the heiress of the wealthy Carl Masterson, streams of people filed through the Masterson home, claiming him as family. Devon and a Laramie police officer stood guard at the front door, turning away anyone who was rude, hostile, or dressed sloppily.

"Shawn is polite, well-mannered, and well-dressed," said Carl. "He didn't get that way by accident. If someone passes that inspection, show them in to me, and I will evaluate their proof."

Few people got in to see Carl Masterson, and those who did couldn't prove any relation to Shawn. Reporters set up their cameras inside Mr. Masterson's gate, shooting random footage, but they failed to capture a reunion on film. By the next morning, Shawn's story and picture reached the front page of several community newspapers.

A ringing telephone roused Randy from a restless slumber. He would have slept better had Tracy been home, but she'd been so hurt by his dishonesty that she promptly packed up their boys and went to stay with her sister in Cheyenne.

Still half asleep, Randy fumbled with the phone and nearly knocked it off the nightstand before getting the receiver to his ear. "Yeah."

"Randy, this is Calvin. I'm glad I caught you."

"Where else would I be at seven thirty in the morning? I lost my job, and I'm awaiting a hearing which will determine the number of charges that the police department intends to file against me for our little bonus program. I thought you got arrested, too."

"I'm out on bond, same as you. Listen, I know it's early, but a unique and profitable opportunity has just landed in our laps."

"Oh?"

"Guess who's on the front page of this morning's newspaper?"

"Who?"

"Shawn. Remember him telling you that he's between girlfriends?"

"Yeah."

"Well, he's *not* between girlfriends. He's engaged to the daughter of the *very* wealthy Carl Masterson. And guess what, bud? He has amnesia. They're trying to locate his family."

Randy bolted upright in bed. "Amnesia? Oh, the possibilities. But if Chief McNare sees the paper ..."

"He won't. I talked to Jarrod and threatened to turn him in for his involvement in our little bonus program unless he keeps the chief and captain from seeing the front page of the morning paper."

"I still don't know how Jarrod escaped arrest," said Randy. "I've heard that the chief has a cassette recording implicating you, me, and Scott. But for some reason Jarrod isn't mentioned."

"That is a little strange. Whoever recorded that tape had to know that Jarrod was involved because he was always with us."

"Well, it wasn't Menzo. He got caught on his first job, but Shawn disappeared before we were arrested. Do you suppose he had something to do with our arrest?"

"I don't see how. The only opportunity he had to record us was the day we met at your house for the cook-out, and Jarrod was with us. Tell me that he wouldn't have blown the whistle on Jarrod, too. No. I think he ran when he heard about the tape. He's engaged to a wealthy dame and doesn't need the money from this dumpy job anyway."

Randy nodded in agreement. "That makes sense."

"I'll be over in thirty minutes. Then we'll go to the Masterson estate to pick up our young cousin and cash in on his inheritance. After all, he has no siblings and since his parents were killed in a car wreck, we're all the family he has left."

"You think they'll buy it?" asked Randy.

"Of course. They're desperate to locate that boy's family. We know his whole life history, and what we don't know, we'll make up at the front door. See you in a bit."

Charlene Davarie's boarding house was quiet at this hour. But when she saw the front page of the morning paper, she nearly spilled her coffee. Her eyes riveted from Shawn's picture to the article, and she flew through the story.

Shawn has amnesia, and they're trying to locate his family. Drumming her fingers on the table, Charlene studied his picture. *And he's engaged to Carl Masterson's daughter? That man is incredibly wealthy.*

Laying aside the newspaper, she bounced up and stepped over to the sink, emptying her coffee cup and giving it a quick rinse.

If I can claim Shawn as my son ... oh, the money that could be mine!

Charlene snatched up the telephone and punched in Marisa's phone number. "Marisa, dear, you're not at work?"

"I go in at two. What's up?"

"Do you still have that photo of you and Shawn?"

182

"Of course. It's on my refrigerator door."

"Great. Put the picture in your purse. I just found out that Shawn's in trouble and needs us."

"What kind of trouble?" asked Marissa.

"I'll explain on the way. Just get ready to go, and *don't* forget that picture. I'll be over in twenty minutes."

Erin Shaughnessy finished unloading the dishwasher while her nine-year-old daughter, Stephanie, washed the table and dried it with a dish towel.

"Thanks, Stephie." Seven-year-old Sandy plopped down at the clean table with her coloring book and crayons.

Rinsing the breakfast dishes, Erin neatly stacked them in the dishwasher, all the while thinking of her son.

Take care of him, Lord. Send angels to guard and protect him. I don't think I could go on if I had to bury Skip next to his daddy.

It had been more than three weeks since she'd talked to him. Where was he? Was he in danger? Who was protecting him and keeping him from harm's way? The thought of her nineteen-year-old son carrying a loaded handgun and possibly laying his life on the line to protect someone's *property* worried her when he was home, but he had good friends with the department who looked out for him. Who was taking care of him now?

The voice of her four-year-old daughter broke into her thoughts.

"Here's the paper, Mommy."

"Thanks, Suzi. Put it on the table for me, and I'll read it later."

Sandy looked up from her coloring. "Mom, I miss Skip. When is he coming home?"

"As soon as his assignment is finished, but I don't know when that will be, sweetheart."

With a sorrowful sigh, Erin closed the dishwasher and wiped the counter tops. The telephone rang and she looked at it, afraid to pick it up, afraid that the caller might be from the police department with information about her son – possibly bearing news that she didn't want to hear.

Stephanie answered the ringing telephone. "Hello? ... Just a minute." She looked over at her mother. "Mom, it's Officer Spencer."

Skip's partner. That's all she needed to hear. This one phone call confirmed her worst fear.

"Thank you, Stephie." Erin took a deep breath and reached for the phone. "Hello, Jesse."

"Mrs. Shaughnessy, have you seen the morning paper?"

Baffled by his question, Erin raised an eyebrow. "Uh ... no. Why?"

"Well, um, maybe you'd better stop what you're doing and take a look at it."

"OK. What am I looking for?"

"Just look at the front page. You'll find it. If you need me for anything, don't hesitate to call me back. Bye."

Erin hung up the phone and motioned for Stephanie to hand her the newspaper. "Thank you, dear." She pulled it from the plastic bag and unfolded it.

Her son's picture grabbed her attention. With a gasp, her eyes flew across the caption under it before she skimmed the article.

The Crackpots Emerge

"Mom, what is it?" Stephanie drew close to her mother to see the front page of the paper.

Erin handed her the newspaper and snatched up the phone, punching in Jesse's number. "Jesse, that article says he's been with these people for two days. How did this happen with no one knowing about it?"

"I don't know, and Captain Kramer isn't here. He's out of town and won't be back until late tonight."

"Well, I'm going to Laramie. Will you stay with the girls for me?"

"Sure, I'll be over in thirty minutes."

Erin got ready to go and instructed the girls to behave for Skip's partner. The moment Jesse arrived, she hugged and kissed her daughters. Then she dashed out the door. She dreaded the four-hour drive ahead of her – two hours each direction. But at least the address was printed in the article, so she knew where to go.

Running a household as large as the Masterson estate required a lot of coordinating, so Devon frequently found himself running from the moment he got up in the morning until he fell into bed at night. Fortunately, his first-floor bedroom allowed him easy access to a quick nap during the day.

Widowed at a young age, Devon landed a position with Carl Masterson, vowing never to remarry. He always sought extra tasks to keep him busy – anything to stifle the painful memories of losing his beloved wife and precious son. He adored the triplets, transferring his love for his late son to the three sweet toddlers that lived in the estate, and they became the daughters he never had.

Occasionally, he got caught up playing hide and seek with the girls or reading them stories while his chores sat untouched. That frustrated Carl, but Martha assured him that Devon would get the work done. And he always did. It was that intense responsibility and trustworthiness, combined with Devon's great love for the triplets that eventually got him promoted to the head of Mr. Masterson's staff.

Since he loved the girls like they were his own daughters, it grieved him to see Carl forcing Crystal to marry a violent and bitter man like Michael. And although Devon kept quiet, the girls talked to him, sharing their thoughts and concerns. So it pleased him to learn that Carl had permitted Crystal to call off her engagement with Michael. Crystal credited Shawn.

Standing in the doorway of the recreation room, Devon observed Shawn and Billie interacting on a property trade during a game of Monopoly. Crystal begged her not to trade, while Jayme encouraged Shawn to throw in a railroad to seal the deal.

Devon studied the lad. He was kind and considerate of others, always respectful. The only person who didn't like him was Michael. Levi and Grant both respected him. The girls adored him. Even Carl liked, trusted, and respected him. And Devon knew from experience that any individual who so quickly landed in good with Carl had to be extraordinary.

"Hey, Devon, come join the game," said Crystal. "You haven't played Monopoly with us in a long time."

Still pondering, Devon smiled at the triplets and looked at Shawn again. *Someone has got to be looking for that boy. He has the most endearing personality. If he were my son, I'd be going crazy trying to find him. How come he's not been reported missing? How come that newspaper article only brought out the crackpots and not his family?*

"Devon?" Jayme broke into his thoughts.

"I'd love to play. Thanks." He started into the room, but the doorbell rang. Devon did an about face. "Let me get that first."

Trotting down the stairs and across the lavish entranceway, Devon swung open the front door. A middle-aged woman promptly slapped him with a rolled up newspaper. The young blonde beside her jumped, and her mouth dropped open, obviously surprised.

"I believe you have my son."

"Ma'am?" Devon knew exactly what she wanted, but he found that playing stupid brought out the worst in people, and he was watching for someone who's behavior emulated Shawn's.

"I'm Charlene Da –" The woman snapped open the newspaper and glanced at the front page. "Christopher. Charlene Christopher, and this is my son." She pointed at Shawn's front page photo before sliding her arm around the young lady beside her. "This is Marisa, my daughter. Show him the picture, Marisa."

Marisa blushed as she withdrew the photograph and handed it to Devon. "Mom, what are you doing?" she whispered.

"I take it you see the resemblance?"

A picture indicated that Marissa knew him, but her mother's belligerence raised his guard, especially the way she stumbled over her introduction.

"Yes, Ma'am, I do. They both have blond hair, but I'm afraid that one picture is not sufficient proof for us to release Shawn into your custody. Do you have any other proof that he's your son?"

Of course, you don't. Your name isn't Mrs. Christopher, and you are no relation to him, but some people will do anything for money.

The woman's mouth dropped open. "W-w-well, of course not. I mean ... I mean certainly."

While she stammered out a lame reply, two men trotted up behind her, greeting Devon as if she were invisible.

"Sir, my name is Randy Tidwell, and this is my brother, Calvin. We're so relieved that you found our young cousin. We've been beside ourselves with worry over his disappearance."

"Your cousin!" screamed the woman. "How dare you show up here trying to claim my son as *your* relative!"

Ignoring her outburst, Devon addressed Randy. "You couldn't have been too concerned. You didn't file a missing person's report on him."

"Uh, that's because we didn't realize he was missing," said Calvin. "We saw his picture in the paper."

"Is that a fact? You just said you've been beside yourselves with worry, and now you tell me you didn't realize he was missing. So which is it?"

Randy and Calvin looked at each other, and Devon knew they were trying to think up a quick response.

"The truth is," said Randy. "Right before his parents died, we promised them that we would look after him. So we actually didn't realize he was missing until we saw his picture in the paper and read the article."

"Well, if you've been looking after him, like you claim, how did his disappearance escape your notice? This is the third day he's been with us."

Calvin and Randy exchanged glances. It was obvious to Devon that they hadn't planned their story around this line of questioning.

"Um, look, he is our cousin," said Randy. "We're the only family he has left. Can we at least see him?"

"I'm sorry, Mr. Tidwell. We need proof that you're his family before we will release him into your care."

"Proof?" echoed Calvin.

Devon motioned toward the two women. "As you can see, these ladies also claim him."

Randy glared at the older woman. "You old battleaxe, you used to be his landlady, and you gave him grief." Spinning on his heel, Randy skipped down the steps toward the car. "Come on, Calvin. Let's go find proof that Shawney boy is ours."

The two women reluctantly followed, trudging dejectedly down the marble steps.

Leaning against the doorframe, Devon watched them climb into their separate vehicles and depart, driving down the long driveway. He just shook his head. Now even the people who knew him wanted to exploit him for monetary gain.

Devon sighed. *This is going to be a long day. I'd like to know that someone out there actually cares about him.*

Chapter 26

In Need of Proof

Devon closed the door and returned to the recreation room. He had barely entered the room when the doorbell rang again. He promptly spun around and strode back to the front door.

"How may I help you?" he asked the young couple on the front step. The woman was carrying a baby.

"Please, sir, the newspaper says you have my brother."

"Your brother?" echoed Devin. He looked past the couple to the stragglers climbing the marble steps, hurrying toward the door. Cars cruising up the driveway. People exiting their vehicles.

Oh, boy.

"Shawn, sir. My brother's name is Shawn."

Devon looked at her. "Yes, of course. If you'll wait here, I'll be right back. I think I need a little help to deal with this crowd."

Devon notified Carl, who called the Laramie PD and requested they send over an officer. But until he arrived, Devon did the best he could to interview the people who arrived to claim Shawn.

The young couple was gracious and left without altercation. And so did several others when they couldn't produce proof that they were related to Shawn. But some people were rude and hostile, so Devon had them wait until the police got there.

He'd been standing at the door for almost two hours without a break when the last person in line finally drove away.

"I got to go," said the officer. "If you need me, don't hesitate to call."

"Thanks, Jon." Devon shook his hand. "I'll take you up on that."

While the police car was pulling out, a mint green minivan turned in.

Devon leaned against the doorframe of the extra wide doorway. The woman slid from her van and approached him. Fidgeting with the newspaper, she smiled nervously.

Great, here comes another crackpot trying to use that boy as a means to wealth. Jon left a tad too early. "Yes, Ma'am. What can I do for you?"

"My name is Erin Shaughnessy." The nicely dressed lady unfolded the newspaper and held it up. "According to this article, you have my son, although the newspaper has his name wrong. His name is Skip Shaughnessy."

"Can you prove it?"

Erin raised an eyebrow. "Can I prove his name is wrong?"

I could have worded that better.

"No, I don't have his ID on me, but I have a family photo in my wallet, which should prove he's my son."

Wonderful! If she has a family photo, I would feel comfortable letting her in to see him.

Erin searched her purse and wallet. "Oh, no. Suzi's been in my purse again. I can't find it. Look, he is my son."

"Where do you live?"

"Forest Valley, and I've driven almost two hours to get here."

"May I see your driver's license?" *Shawn's license was issued in Forest Valley. Now if they just have the same address ...*

"Certainly, but what good does that do?" Erin handed him her license.

Devon glanced down at her license, and his heart sank. The addresses didn't match, but something in her manner suggested that this woman might, indeed, be Shawn's mother. Yet so many people had attempted to falsely claim him that he thought it best to require proof positive, something she'd have in her possession if she were really his mother.

"Ma'am, if you'll wait here, I'll be right back." Devon closed the door and hurried to Carl's office. "Mr. Masterson, there is a woman at the front door who's claiming Shawn is her son."

"Does she have proof?" asked Carl.

Devon handed him her driver's license. "Not with her, but she is from Forest Valley. She told me that the newspaper has his name wrong. She said his name is Skip."

Carl examined her driver's license and handed it back to Devon. "She has a street address on her license. He has a box number. She's just another crackpot, Devon. Get rid of her."

"Yes, sir." Devon returned to the front porch and handed Erin her driver's license. "I'm sorry, Ma'am, but we need proof positive before we will release him to you."

"I understand. May I see him before I leave? I am his mother and shall return tomorrow with proof, but I'd feel better if I could see he's all right."

"Ma'am, I assure you, he has received the best of care. However, Mr. Masterson is not allowing anyone to see him without proof because many people have attempted to falsely claim him."

"Are you serious?" gasped Erin.

"Unfortunately, I am." Devon motioned behind her. "See for yourself."

Erin turned around. Cars streamed into the driveway and several people were already approaching the front door. One young woman held up the newspaper and pointed at the front-page photo of Shawn.

"This my little brother," she said, smacking gum as she talked. "And you ain't got no right to keep him here. My folks is worried sick about him."

"I suppose you have proof that he's your brother?" asked Devon.

"Yeah, I do." The woman thrust a three-by-five snapshot into his hand.

Erin's eyes widened.

Devon examined the picture and handed it back. *At least his landlady had a recent photo of him.* "Ma'am, this does not qualify as proof, I'm afraid. This is a baby picture."

"Whatcha talkin' about? That's me when I was four and that's Shawn when he was one. Now, let him go, or I'll call the police."

Devon sighed as more people fell into line. "Uh, don't bother. I'll save you the trouble and call them myself." Turning to Erin, he said, "I'm sorry I can't allow you to see him, but now you see why."

"And who is she?" demanded the young woman.

"She's his mother."

"Ridiculous. I'm his sister and I've never seen her before."

Erin smiled at Devon. "Thank you for protecting Skip from all this. I'll be back tomorrow with proof."

Now that's the second time she referred to him as Skip. Where have I heard that name before?

The moment Erin turned to leave, the noise level on the porch rose as people competed for Devon's attention, clamoring to be next in line.

Devon sighed. *This is going to be another long day.* "Excuse me one moment," he said. "I'll be right back."

He quietly closed the door and strolled into the kitchen to phone the police. "Mr. Masterson, we have more people here wanting custody of Shawn."

"Is that woman causing trouble?" asked Carl.

"No. She seemed genuine. She was polite and well dressed. She appeared most concerned about his well-being and assured me that she would return tomorrow with evidence that he is her son."

"We'll see," said Carl. "According to his driver's license, his name is Shawn. What did she call him?"

"Skip." Devon snapped his fingers. "That's what Billie was calling him. She insisted that he introduced himself as Skip."

Carl raised an eyebrow. "That's right."

"Shall I run after her, sir?"

"No. She promised to return tomorrow with proof. Having proof will set our minds at ease that he is, in fact, her son and that she's not another gold digger."

When Erin arrived home, Jesse was watching television with the girls, Scooter in his lap.

"What happened?" he asked. "Where's Skip?"

"They wouldn't let me see him. Apparently, people from all over have been lining up at their front door trying to claim him for one reason or another."

Jesse's mouth fell open. "You're kidding!

"No. I was there when people showed up demanding that Carl Masterson release him into their custody, so they're requiring proof that I'm his mother. And I will have proof when I return tomorrow."

"Do you want me to keep the girls for you again?"

Erin smiled. "No, Jesse. They are part of my proof."

Jesse stood and set Scooter on the sofa. "Oh, before I forget, Cassandra's mom called for you. She saw Skip's picture and the article in the paper this morning."

"Oh, my gosh! I completely forgot to call Anita about this. Thank you." Erin reached for the phone as Jesse slipped out the front door.

On the second ring, Anita's anxious voice shot over the phone line. "Erin. Did you get Skip? Is he OK?"

With a sigh, Erin sank onto the sofa and pulled Scooter into a hug. "I don't know. I didn't get to see him. They want proof that I'm his mother, so I'm going back to Laramie tomorrow morning with proof."

"That's an incredibly long drive. Would you like us to keep the girls for you?"

"Actually, no. I would like to take Cassandra with us. Is that possible?"

"She would love it. All she's done is sit around the house for the past three weeks pining for Skip. Do you want me to drop her off on my way to work?

199

"No, we'll pick her up, or I'll arrange a ride for her. Thanks, Anita."

That evening, Erin gathered recent photos of Skip with his sisters. She rummaged through his dresser drawer, locating his current driver's license and police department photo ID card. Then she phoned the station and left a message for Captain Kramer to call her as soon as possible, regardless of the time. He returned her call just before midnight.

"Erin, I'm sorry to call so late. What's the problem?"

"Paul, have you talked to the Kenton Police Department about Skip's assignment?"

"No, I haven't. For me to call down there could blow his cover."

"I assume you haven't seen today's paper."

"As a matter of fact, I haven't. Why?"

"Go look at the front page and call me back." Without waiting for a reply, she hung up.

Minutes later, the phone rang. Erin snatched it up on the first ring. "Well, Paul?"

"Oh, Erin, I don't know what to say. They were supposed to call me when his assignment was through."

"I went to Laramie this afternoon. Without proof that he's my son, they wouldn't even let me see him. Well, tomorrow, I'm going back to Laramie with proof that Skip is my son, and I want you to go with me."

"Absolutely. Make sure you have his valid ID with you."

"I've already grabbed it."

"Good. I'll be by to get you and the girls around eight o'clock."

"Would you stop at the McKenzie's house on the way and pick up Cassandra?"

"I'd be delighted. What's her address?"

The Voice of Reason

Up and running by seven o'clock, Carl Masterson summoned Kenny. "I need you to run an errand for me."

"What about Shawn?"

"Take him with you, unless, of course, he's still asleep."

"He is."

"This won't take long, but it's time-sensitive and needs to be done immediately. I'm sure he'll be all right during the short time you're gone."

Sitting in his car in the driveway of the Masterson estate, Michael glanced at his watch. It was seven o'clock. He suspected that the house was already a bustle of activity because breakfast was served promptly at eight, and Carl was a stickler for promptness.

Why am I here? That was a dumb question. He intended to shake some sense into Crystal.

Michael studied the house, considering his best course of action. Should he go to the door and try to talk to her, or should he leave?

That rotten, no-good creep that's staying here influenced her against me. If I ever get my hands on him...

His mind raced back to the fistfight with Shawn.

With two guys holding him, he still clobbered me. What I need is something to give me an edge.

A pleasant thought burst into his mind. Michael smiled and reached for the glove box, popping open the small door. Out rolled a pocket-size cylinder of mace.

"This has been in the glove box since the day I bought it. I don't know why I left it in there, but it'll come in handy today."

Sliding from his vehicle, Michael dropped the cylinder into his trouser pocket and closed his car door. He stood beside the car and lit a cigarette. Puffing furiously, he attempted to squelch the uneasy feeling of entering Carl's home uninvited, while nurturing his justifiable anger and hostility toward the man who'd stolen his woman.

Michael started pacing. Every step he took increased his fury. Just the thought of Shawn's charming smile and courteousness made him ill.

He saved Crystal from drowning, and they all think he's a hero. Well, he's nothin' and I'll prove it.

He trotted around the house to the side service entrance, which was frequently unlocked during the day, and resumed pacing, still puffing on his cigarette. Collecting his courage, he pushed open the door and peeked inside. No one in sight. He started to toss his cigarette away but changed his mind.

No smoking in the house. I hate that rule. No one will ever know.

Cigarette in hand, Michael slipped into the house and up the stairs. He peered around the corner. Taking a quick puff, he stole down the hallway, up another flight of stairs, and headed for the third-floor guest rooms.

The hallway was deserted. Michael tiptoed down the corridor and peeked into each room, looking for Shawn's. The doors stood wide open, which made the rooms easy to check. When he reached the second guest room, the door was closed. Glancing both ways, he turned the knob and pushed it open. There lay Shawn, sound asleep.

With a cocky smirk, Michael stepped into the room, closed the door, and locked it behind him.

Billie tapped on Crystal's bedroom door before turning the knob and pushing it open. "You ready? We want to get out of here before everyone's up."

Crystal shook her head. "Come in and close the door. I'm not dressed yet."

JJ followed Billie into her sister's room and shut the door. "Billie, I'm not sure that this is a good idea.

Remember what happened the last time we tried to sneak off to see Tim and Danny?"

"Yeah, but this time Crystal's going with us."

"Dad will miss us at breakfast."

"You think? Yesterday morning, by seven thirty, people were already lined up on our front porch. We were all late for breakfast. I suspect that this morning will be a repeat of yesterday. By the time Mom and Dad start to miss us, we'll be back."

Michael glanced around the room, puffing on his cigarette to calm his nerves. But when Shawn started coughing, he whipped it behind his back and waved his hand to clear the air.

Studying Shawn, Michael took one last draw on his cigarette and strolled over to the bed. There were no ashtrays in the room, so he balanced the lighted cigarette on the edge of the dresser. Michael crammed his hands into his pockets and fingered the small can of mace.

I'm ready this time. He stepped to the right side of Shawn's bed.

Shawn rubbed his eyes and rolled to his stomach. Pushing his pillow aside, he rested his head on the mattress. Michael froze, holding his breath to keep from making the slightest sound. Shawn lay with one arm at his side and the other one by his head.

This is it. He'll wish he never messed with me. He seized Shawn's arm and yanked him off the bed, slugging him in the stomach and back-fisting him across the face.

Shawn tumbled backwards into the dresser, rocking it and falling to the soft shag carpet. Clutching his stomach and gasping for breath, he struggled to his feet.

Michael kicked his feet out from under him, and he hit the floor hard. As Shawn started to get up again, Michael swung at him repeatedly. Finally on his feet, Shawn ducked and dodged his fist, tripping over the draperies.

"Let's see you avoid this!" Pulling the mace from his pocket, Michael sprayed it in his eyes.

"Ahhhhh!" Shawn clapped his hands over his eyes and dropped to his knees, but Michael wrenched him to his feet.

"You want Crystal?" He slammed Shawn against the door and slugged him again and again. "You ... can ... have ... her." Michael belted him with each word.

Shawn crumpled to the floor near the door. Michael gasped at what he'd done. He knelt beside Shawn and felt for a pulse.

Closing Crystal's bedroom door behind them, the girls tiptoed down the stairs.

"What was that noise?" asked Billie.

"What noise?"

"I heard a thud. Didn't either of you hear it?"

207

"You're imagining things," said Crystal. "Let's get out of here before we get caught."

"It came from upstairs. Shawn's upstairs. Let's go check on him and make sure he's OK. Maybe he had another bad dream and fell out of bed or something."

Michael leaped to his feet, his fury melting into dread. *Oh, God, I didn't mean to hit him so hard.* Shawn lay unconscious on the floor. Nearby, flames crept up the draperies and leaped to the ruffled bed skirt. His cigarette! *Or start a fire.*

A thought popped into his head. *It's small. You can easily smother it and beat it out.*

No! Oh, no! I've got to get out of here. His breathing rapid and shallow, Michael rubbed sweaty palms on his jeans. Stepping over Shawn, he opened the bedroom door, re-locked it, and quietly shut it behind him, drowning out the voice of reason.

Shawn was innocent, and in his heart, Michael knew nothing had happened between Shawn and Crystal. He wasn't being fair to Shawn or to Crystal, and he'd just abandoned the lad in a burning building, leaving him to die. But Michael had to get out *now!*

Chapter 28

Among the Missing

Michael bolted toward the stairs. His heart nearly stopped when he heard the triplets jogging up the steps. Changing direction, he darted down the hallway and ducked into another room, listening at the closed door. The girls tapped on Shawn's bedroom door.

"Shawn, are you all right?" called Billie.

Michael heard the doorknob rattle, but the girls couldn't get in because he'd locked the door.

Why did I lock that door? They could save him. And he'd tell them what happened, and they'd tell their father, and ... and ... Oh, man, if Carl finds out, I'm dead. Maybe it's better this way.

Coward.

Michael pushed the intrusive thought aside. He was a coward, and he knew it.

Billie's voice interrupted his thoughts. "Do you smell something burning?"

Crystal laughed. "It's probably your brain. You burned it up thinking too much."

"Be serious, Crystal. Don't you smell something?"

"No. Now let's leave before we wake Shawn. He probably locked his door to keep us from doing just that."

The girls ran down the stairs, and the sound of their footsteps faded. Now alone, Michael started to open the door, but he caught sight of another exit on the far side of the room. He grinned with relief. *Yes! Much safer to take another way out. Less chance of running into anyone.*

Crossing the room, he slipped out the other door and trotted down the back hallway. This was a section of the house he had never been in. He wandered the halls, ducking and hiding from Carl Masterson's staff as they went about their duties. With a sigh of defeat, he realized he was hopelessly lost.

The smoke and fire set off an alarm that sounded throughout the entire manor. Michael heard the alarm and expected that, by now, the fire department was en route and evacuation procedures well underway. Since he no longer spotted any of Carl's staff, he could only guess that they had already left the premises.

Shawn choked, gasping for a wisp of untainted air.

Fire!

Unable to breathe and at the point of panic, he groped for the door, finally locating the knob. A blistering hot pain scorched the palm of his right hand and he jerked his hand back. Stripping off his pajama shirt, he wrapped it around the doorknob and turned it. A faint click unlocked the door, and he yanked it open. Smoke poured into the hallway. The sudden rush of oxygen livened the flames and they leapt at the door, catching fire to his shirt.

Overwhelmed by the immense heat, coughing so hard he choked, Shawn staggered into the smoke-filled hallway and pulled the door shut behind him. Although there were no flames in the hallway, the thick smoke made it difficult to see and impossible to breathe.

Disoriented by the smoke, he stumbled blindly into a closed door. Shawn wanted to escape the fire anyway he could, so he pulled open the door and limped into the deserted room. He closed the door behind him. Still coughing hard, Shawn leaned wearily against the closed door and slid down to the floor. He coughed uncontrollably for two minutes.

Finally able to catch his breath, he wondered why his bedroom door had been locked. He never locked that door, although a locked door would have prevented Michael from entering while he was sleeping. Shawn started coughing again.

Hey, where was Kenny when Michael barged into my room and assaulted me? And did Michael purposely lock the door to prevent anyone from finding me?

Recovered from another coughing spasm, Shawn glanced across the room and spotted another exit. Dragging himself to his feet, he crossed the room and hobbled through the other door.

It hurt to breathe, and it hurt to move.

He paused in the doorway, thinking, remembering the back door that Kenny had showed him during his tour of the house.

Now, if I can remember how to get there, I'll be OK.

Coughing again, Shawn held his stomach. And it hurt to cough.

Sirens pierced the morning silence. On the highway into Laramie, two fire trucks and an ambulance sped past the girls headed the opposite direction.

Billie pulled onto the shoulder of the road. "You don't suppose that was Tim and Danny?"

"Well, they are firefighters," said Crystal.

The triplets drove into town and headed for the apartment that the two friends shared. They knocked loudly on the door, but no one answered.

Billie glanced around the serene building. "That *was* them."

"Great," moaned JJ. "We finally manage to sneak away to see them and they're not home. Let's go. If we hurry, we'll be on time for breakfast."

The fire spread fast. Michael was no longer concerned with getting out unnoticed. He just wanted to get out. Then he realized he didn't know *how* to get out. He was lost, and panic gripped him.

He darted from room to room, looking for an exit. In his haste, he tripped and tumbled down a flight of stairs. Momentarily dazed, he sat up, rubbing his head.

Beginning to hyperventilate, Michael brought his hand to his chest, wheezing with each breath. He grasped the banister and tried to pull himself up.

"Aaaah! My ankle!"

An intense pain shot through his right ankle, and he collapsed.

Shawn's bedroom window shattered, and flames erupted from it. Firefighters shot water up to the third floor through the window, dousing the raging flames.

The fire chief approached Carl. "Mr. Masterson, is everyone out of the house?"

"No! My three daughters are still inside, and so is a friend of ours."

"As far as you know, everyone else got out."

"Yes, yes, everyone else is accounted for. Please, you have to save them. My daughters are on the second floor, and Shawn is on the third."

Fully suited up, four firefighters entered Carl's expansive manor to search for the missing.

Shawn coughed and choked on the smoky haze that infiltrated the house. Although he saw no flames, the house was so hot, he suspected the fire was on the other side of the wall.

Recalling all that Kenny had shown him on his recent tour of Carl's manor, he headed for the nearby stairway, hobbling down the stairs. Halfway down, he stifled a cough and jerked to a stop. There sat Michael – on the floor at the bottom of the steps.

"Help me, please," begged Michael. "I fell, and I'm hurt."

Shawn was in no condition to handle another confrontation with Michael. He could hardly walk. He was bruised and sore, and he'd been burned. A single blow might incapacitate him, and he feared that Michael would slug him again. Swallowing hard, Shawn slowly backed up the stairs.

"Don't leave me! Please. I'm hurt."

Shawn paused. Michael couldn't identify him, but genuine despair laced his voice. And he couldn't abandon someone in need, regardless of past conflicts between them. Stifling a cough, he cautiously started down the stairs.

"Thank you," wheezed Michael. "I promise to repay your kindness. I think I broke my ankle and a couple of ribs. I'm having trouble breathing."

Shawn started coughing again. *Me, too.* He stepped onto the cool tile floor. Kneeling beside Michael, he slid his arm around him and helped him to stand.

Michael groaned in pain. "Thank you." He looked at Shawn and gasped. "Shawn, are you OK?"

No. It hurts to breath and it hurts to move, but then, you weren't happy until you put me into this condition.

Shawn didn't reply. He concentrated on finding the way out before the fire reached them.

Turning up their endless driveway, Crystal said, "What's going on?

The girls gasped. Flames erupted from the third story windows. They parked as close to the gate as the emergency vehicles permitted, and they dashed between two police officers toward the house.

"Whoa!" An officer stopped them. "You can't go in there."

"Where's Shawn?" Billie frantically glanced around. "Did he get out?"

Hearing their voices, Carl and Martha rushed to their daughters.

"Oh, thank goodness you're safe!" Martha gathered them into a warm embrace. "We thought you'd been trapped."

"Mom, where's Shawn?"

"I don't know, dear. He must still be inside."

Tears pooled in Billie's eyes and trickled down her cheeks. And while the Masterson family watched helplessly as flames devoured part of their home, Billie wept, fearful for Shawn's safety.

Despite her van-load of proof that Skip was her son, Erin couldn't shake the uneasy feeling that it wouldn't be sufficient. And she *had* to see him, to touch him, to know that he was all right.

She worried about him, and it had just about killed her to watch him leave for that undercover assignment. In fact, she had tried to stop him from going, although Skip didn't know that. She appealed to Chief Clark and Captain Kramer, begging them to send someone else, anyone but her innocent son.

She didn't want him to get hurt. Jesse wouldn't be there to protect him. And she didn't want him corrupted like the cops he was supposed to catch. She relied heavily on him. If anything happened to Skip, she would fall apart.

The Forest Valley police van pulled up to the gate. Cassandra gasped, and Erin's eyes widened at the sight of fire trucks, and a twinge of dread pierced her heart.

Uh – oh.

With an envelope of documents and pictures, she slid out of the van. Cassandra stepped down and helped Skip's little sisters jump out.

Erin took Suzi's small hand while Cassandra scooped up the youngest, and they trailed Captain Paul Kramer to the gate. Sandy and Stephanie brought up the rear.

A Laramie police officer stopped them. Dressed neatly in his Forest Valley uniform, Paul explained why they had come.

The officer sighed. "Look folks, I can sympathize with you, but you've come at a bad time."

"Is everyone out of the house?" asked Erin. "I'm looking for my son. Here's his picture."

The officer pursed his lips and studied the photo. Glancing back at the burning building, he shook his head. "I'm sorry. I overheard one of the Masterson girls say that he's still inside."

Erin's head started spinning, and Paul grasped her arm to steady her. "Oh, Paul." Releasing Suzi, she melted into his arms, sobbing uncontrollably.

"Ma'am, do you have proof that he's your son?" asked the officer.

Erin wiped her eyes and nodded. Within a minute, she had the patrolman convinced, and he let them through. Knowing Skip was still inside, there was nothing to do but wait and pray.

Chapter 29

All the Facts

Carl and his wife stared at their blazing home in horror. The fire chief approached them, interrupting their thoughts.

"Mr. Masterson, we have the fire under control. It appeared to have started in one of the third-floor guest rooms."

"How do you know that?" asked Carl.

"That's where the damage is the worst, but we'll know more after the investigation."

"Thank you." With a frown, Carl looked at his wife. "Did you hear what he said? The fire started in a third-floor guestroom, and Shawn's the only guest we have. He started that fire!"

With the soft smile known for turning away his wrath, Martha said, "Oh, Carl, why would he do such a thing?"

"I don't know, Martha, but who else could have done it?"

"Maybe it was an electrical fire, started by a faulty appliance or a short in the wiring."

"The last time the fire department inspected, they found no potential hazards. *None.* All the evidence points to Shawn, and remember, we hardly know him. I hate to admit it, but Michael was right about him. I'll see to it that he's charged with arson."

"My son doesn't start fires. He did not do it."

Carl turned to face the woman speaking. "What do you mean, your son? Who are you, and where did you come from?"

"My name is Erin Shaughnessy. That boy is my son, and I can prove it."

"Good!" cried Carl. "Because I hold you personally responsible for my property damage. Now, get off my property!"

"I'm not leaving without Skip. You have no right to keep him here. None!"

"You are trespassing!"

"Come on, Erin. We have no choice but leave." A uniformed police captain from another department drew her aside.

Carl caught sight of the Forest Valley patch on his shirt sleeve.

"No! I'm not leaving without knowing what's happened to Skip." Tears trickled down her cheeks.

"It'll be OK. We'll run over to the Laramie PD and return with a police escort."

Carl studied her little party, looking from one child to another. Faces wet with tears, these blonde-haired little angels looked a lot like Shawn.

Martha looped her arm through her husband's. "Let them stay, Carl. Shawn's still inside the house, and she's worried about him, like we worry about our girls."

Shawn started coughing again. The longer he remained inside the building, the more difficulty he had breathing. His lungs desperately needed some pure air.

"I think I know where we are." He struggled to formulate his words because his throat was so scratchy. "Unless I'm mistaken, we're close to the back door."

Wearing only pajama bottoms, Shawn felt blistered from the heat, and it hurt to have Michael's arm around his neck. Hobbling through the hallway with Michael leaning on him heavily, Shawn rounded a sharp corner and nearly ran into the back door. He pushed open the door and shivered at the rush of a cool gust. Instantly chilled by the breeze, Shawn stepped outside into the fresh, untainted air.

He grimaced when Michael stumbled in the doorway and nearly knocked him down. A simple touch to his burning skin sent a stabbing pain through him, yet Michael practically wanted to be carried. He hurt badly enough without the added weight of someone leaning on him for support. And the longer he supported Michael, the more heavily Michael leaned into him. But he couldn't dump him here. They were on the backside of the manor. Not one person in sight.

Shawn helped Michael around the corner of the building. In one broad sweep, his eyes took in everything. The police. Rescue squads and fire trucks. Firefighters swarmed everywhere. The triplets and their parents. But who ... He jerked to a sudden stop and zeroed in on his family.

Mom. His memory came flooding back like a tidal wave.

Then he spotted his fiancée carrying his three-year-old sister.

Cassandra. Her long, auburn hair draped neatly over her shoulders, her slender figure donned in blue jeans and wearing *his* light-brown corduroy jacket. What a beautiful sight she was to him.

"Shawn, what's the matter?" asked Michael.

"Skip!" cried Cassandra. Dropping Scooter into Paul's arms, she bolted past the emergency personnel toward him.

Skip smiled. "Nothing."

The first to reach them, Cassandra threw her arms around his neck and embraced him.

Skip gasped and withdrew from all physical contact. "Ahhh! D-d-don't touch me, Cassandra." He winced from the intense pain.

She released him and stepped back. "Skip, your skin is so hot, but you're shivering."

Catching up with Cassandra, the others surrounded Skip and Michael.

"Michael! What are you doing here?" exclaimed Carl.

Michael grimaced and collapsed into the arms of rescue personnel.

Carl looked at Skip. "Oh, my."

"Skip!"

Three excited little girls charged through the emergency personnel and flung their arms around him. Skip lost his balance and toppled backward into the arms of two paramedics. The paramedics wrapped him in a soft cotton blanket before strapping him to a gurney. Four-year-old Suzi burst into tears and ran into her mother's arms.

"Suzi." Straining to talk, Skip reached for her. "Come here."

Suzi wiped her eyes and shuffled over to him.

Skip clasped her hand. "Be a big girl and help Mom with Scooter until I come home. Okay?"

"When are you coming home?"

"Soon." He spoke barely above a whisper. His eyes dropped shut and his grip loosened.

With a frown, Carl jammed his hands into his trouser pockets, watching the young child. Tears trickled down her cheeks, and she kissed Shawn. The boy's eyes dropped shut and his grip loosened. Her mother pulled her out of the way as the paramedics slid an oxygen mask over his nose and mouth and wheeled the gurney to the ambulance.

Glancing around at the cluster of people milling about, Carl caught sight of an ambulance leaving his property, undoubtedly hauling Michael to the hospital. He turned toward Shawn, but the paramedics had already lifted the gurney into the back of the ambulance. Determined to talk to him, Carl yanked open the back door and started to climb in after him.

"I'm sorry, sir, but you can't go in the ambulance." The paramedic closed the emergency vehicle's rear door again.

"I've got to talk to him," snapped Carl. "Young man, do you know who I am?"

"No, sir, but it doesn't matter. You're not allowed to interfere with our job. Now, if you'll excuse me, we have to get him to the hospital." The paramedic slid into the ambulance, and the vehicle maneuvered down and out of Carl's driveway.

With pursed lips, Carl stared after the ambulance, hands on his hips.

Erin Shaughnessy approached him. "Sir, I don't know what happened here this morning, but my son did not start that fire."

"And how do you know that?"

"Because Skip would never do such a thing. *Never.*"

Crystal approached Erin. "Skip. That's a cute nickname."

"That's not a nickname," said the young woman with Erin. "That *is* his name."

Carl raised an eyebrow.

"See!" exclaimed Billie. "I told you that his name is Skip."

"Who are you?" asked Jayme. "His sister?"

"Cassandra McKenzie. I'm his fiancée."

Crystal gasped. "Shawn's engaged?"

"His name is Skip. And, yes, he's engaged."

Carl turned to Erin. "Ma'am, despite everything that's happened this morning, I still want proof that he's your son. According to his driver's license, his name is Shawn Christopher."

The police captain extended his hand toward him, and Carl grasped it in a firm handshake. "Captain Paul Kramer, Forest Valley Police Department. The license in Skip's possession was issued for a purpose. It's not his real license, and all the information on it is fictitious."

Billie cocked her head. "Even his birth date?"

Captain Kramer nodded. "Afraid so. Skip is only nineteen."

Erin handed Carl her son's valid driver's license. His eyes widened. It looked just as authentic as the one in Shawn's possession. One was phony.

"Okay. Now tell me *why* he was issued a fake license."

Erin handed him a police shield and a police department picture ID

"That kid's a cop?" Carl examined the boy's identification. "He's so young."

"And a sharp dresser," said Martha.

Billie got starry-eyed. "Charming and irresistible." Her sisters gaped at her.

Ignoring his daughter's growing infatuation, Carl handed Shawn's ID back to his mother. "Well- mannered and courteous. He doesn't use bad language like the cops I know."

"No, he doesn't," said Captain Kramer. "Skip has a strong faith in God, and he works hard to please God in all he does. Trust me. He did not start that fire."

"Somebody did, and since the fire broke out in his room, he's my prime suspect."

"I understand. Just don't railroad an innocent person in your frustration." Paul turned to Erin. "We certainly hadn't counted on anything like this, and I need to get back to Forest Valley. Since our plans have changed, what are your intentions?"

"I think we'll get a hotel room near the hospital, so we can be near Skip."

"Then I'll get you and the girls a room at the hotel nearest the hospital. And we should be able to get in touch with a rental car company from there. The department will pay for everything."

"I think not," said Martha. "You and the girls will stay with us while Shawn is in the hospital."

A look of shock crossed Erin's face. "Oh, no. I wouldn't think of imposing."

"No imposition at all. I insist."

"Well ..." Erin's brow creased. "We didn't come prepared to stay for any length of time. I intended to pick up Skip and go home."

"Not a problem," said Martha. "Here's what we'll do. Crystal will take you to the hospital to see Skip, get an update on his condition, and talk to the doctor. Then, you all come back here for lunch. After lunch, I'll have Grant run you home to pack what you and the children will need for a short stay. Since Skip's room was destroyed in the fire, you might want to grab him a few things, as well. How does that sound?"

"You're sure it's no imposition?"

Martha took her hand. "Quite sure, dear."

If there were any doubt in Carl's mind that Erin were truly Skip's mother, her thoughtful consideration of his family just removed it. So how could he possibly believe that her son started the fire when that very notion went against everything he knew in his heart? This boy nearly drowned in an effort to rescue his daughter. Nonetheless, Carl made decisions based on facts and statistics, not intuition or perception. And the facts all pointed to Skip's guilt.

Chapter 30

A Sinking Battleship

It surprised Michael to be admitted to the hospital for observation, especially since he suffered only a broken ankle and mild smoke inhalation. But the doctor wanted to ensure that his shortness of breath cleared up. Although his room was equipped to handle two patients, currently it held only one bed, so Michael found his room unbearably quiet.

Before cancer took her last breath, his mother had warned him that if he didn't get his anger under control, one day it would sink his battleship. With his parents dead and his sister estranged, Michael clung to the only family he had – the Mastersons. Carl treated him like a son and had pushed Crystal into their marriage engagement. So when Crystal boldly called off their wedding, Michael wondered if she had managed to obtain her father's blessing over that decision. If she did, where did that place him in relation to the family?

Now he had that fire to consider. Why didn't he stamp out that smoldering cigarette before the draperies caught fire, or more responsibly, simply honored Carl's 'no smoking' rule and snuffed out his cigarette before entering the house. Then none of this would have happened.

What infuriated him like this? Was it the attention that Crystal gave Shawn?

She never looks at me that way.

And Shawn didn't return her affection, so what drove him to blame the boy? To enter Carl's house illegally? To break the 'no smoking' rule? To assault and abandon an innocent person in a burning building, leaving him to die? To run like a coward, rather than smother the flames that *he'd caused?*

He felt replaced, plain and simple. Without even trying, Shawn had stolen Carl's heart, and Carl now favored *him.*

Michael hated to admit it, but Shawn was right about him. He *was* a coward.

A coward fought dirty. The only way that he could defeat Shawn in a fistfight was to have someone else restrain him, to assault him at a moment when he was most vulnerable, and to wield weapons that he couldn't defend himself against, especially half asleep. And after all that, *Shawn came to his aid.*

What caliber of man was Michael? He was bitter and angry. He had inherited twenty-five million dollars from his father and led Carl to believe that he earned that money through stock trading. Yet, he wasn't even certain that his father had amassed his riches honestly.

For years, his anger grew as he watched his father beat his mother and older sister, Misty. And just like his father beat up the defenseless, he managed to strip Shawn of his defenses, beating him the same way. Michael's greatest heartache was watching his beloved mother die a slow agonizing death after living a painful, agonizing life with an abusive husband.

When he was fourteen, his world crumbled. His mom died. Misty ran away from home with her boyfriend. His dad gave him everything but the one thing he needed most – his time. And Michael felt abandoned.

The next time he saw Misty was five years later at their dad's funeral. She desired to reconcile with him, but pride and sudden wealth erased all the heartache and torment he'd witnessed over the years. His father had never raised a hand against him and left him sole heir to his fortune.

Michael learned later that Misty and her husband struggled financially. They had a sick baby who needed open-heart surgery. Misty regretted sneaking off in the middle of the night without telling him goodbye, but she feared their father would eventually beat her to death. And to protect him from their dad's wrath, she kept her whereabouts secret, afraid for his safety. Once their dad was dead, she no longer had to hide.

Yet, at the funeral, Michael boasted of his wealth, slandered Misty in front of his friends, and implied that he wouldn't give her a dime if she begged for it. He told everyone that she was unworthy of even knowing him. That was the last time he saw her – ten years ago. And his mother's prophecy was coming true. His constant anger had sunk his battleship.

He now had no family or friends. His fiancée dumped him. He started a fire, which did extensive damage to the third floor of the Masterson estate.

When Carl finds out that I'm responsible, he'll have me thrown in jail.

His door opened, and a technician maneuvered a bed through the doorway to the other side of the room. "You have a roommate."

Expecting he wouldn't have a single visitor, Michael smiled. At least he'd have someone to talk to. He looked across the room and his smile faded.

Shawn!

The boy slept on his back, his head turned toward the wall, an IV needle taped to his left arm. And he'd have *lots* of visitors – all the people who'd shun Michael. How ironic that they were roommates.

The technician left the room. A few minutes later, Michael heard voices outside the door.

"Mrs. Shaughnessy, I'm Doctor Cantin. I'm glad I caught you." Her voice was soft and feminine.

"Yes, Dr. Cantin. How's Skip? Will he be all right?"

"I think so. He's been treated for smoke inhalation and burns which cover almost half his body. Most of them are superficial, but some of them are deep, so he may need skin grafting."

Skin grafting. Ouch. He's going to hate me for that, and rightfully so. I caused him to get burned.

Doctor Cantin's voice broke into Michael's thoughts. "We've given him pain medication, combined with a heavy sedative. He's asleep now, but you may go in and see him. I'll check on him this afternoon and again when I make my early-morning rounds."

Sitting up in bed, Michael watched the two ladies and four little girls file into his hospital room and gather around his roommate's bed.

Crystal trailed them into the room. "Michael!" Her eyes darted from Michael to Shawn before joining the others.

"Crystal, I'm sorry for being such a jerk. Will you forgive me?"

"Of course, I forgive you."

Michael's eyes widened in disbelief. Maybe there was hope for this relationship after all.

"But it's over between us."

"Aw, Crystie, how can you say that you forgive me, but that it's over?"

"I forgive you, Michael. We can still be friends. But I won't marry you."

"Fine! Forget I exist. I'm sure that Shawn will make you very happy."

The two ladies at Shawn's bedside exchanged glances.

With a frustrated sigh, Crystal crammed clenched fists into the pockets of her blue jeans. "He's engaged, Michael."

Michael's mouth fell open. "Engaged!"

"Yes! Cassandra is his fiancée." Crystal motioned to the young woman with her. "Now will you drop it all ready?"

"Crystal, I'm ... I'm sorry." Michael swallowed hard. "You'll never know how sorry." Folding his hands in his lap, he looked away.

Shawn's family gathered around his bed, caressing him. Michael watched with resentment, listening while Crystal shared the events of the past few days.

"I'm so sorry, Mrs. Shaughnessy." Crystal's eyes watered. "I'm responsible. And there's no telling how that fire got started."

Michael swallowed hard. She was right. He *wasn't* telling.

"But if I hadn't been speeding in the driveway the other night, none of this would have happened. This is all my fault."

Shawn's mother comforted Crystal with a hug. "You may have hit him with the car, but this part of it wasn't your fault."

Familiar voices drifted through the open door, and the rest of the Masterson family filed in, but Shawn didn't stir.

Heaving a frustrated sigh, Carl glanced from Shawn to Michael. Carl raised an eyebrow, clearly surprised to see him. He stepped beside Michael's bed. "How you doing?"

If you only knew. "I'll be OK. I broke my ankle. And they treated me for mild smoke inhalation. They're only keeping me overnight."

Carl glanced over at the others, clustered around Shawn. Lowering his voice, he spoke barely above a whisper. "What were you doing in my house this morning?"

"Well, um ..." Michael slid down, wanting to crawl under the covers and hide. He had to think up a believable story. He couldn't tell Carl the truth. "I came to apologize to Crystal."

Carl raised a questioning eyebrow. "You? Apologize? Unbelievable. Did you at any time go near Shawn's room on the third floor? I was wondering if you heard or saw anything."

Michael shook his head.

"Well, I plan to talk to him when he wakes up."

"T-t-talk to him? Ab-b-bout what?"

"About starting that fire. The fire originated in his room, and he was the only one in there. Who else could have done it?"

Michael bit his lower lip and glanced over at his sleeping roommate. Shawn was about to be accused of something he didn't do, but the evidence was circumstantial. If he fought the charge, he'd be acquitted, and no one would know what had actually happened. No one, except Michael, and he would never tell.

Chapter 31

Falsely Accused

Damage from the fire was confined mainly to the third floor. Although parts of the second and fourth floors had suffered, there was plenty of livable space to house everyone.

The moment the family returned home, Martha sent the servants through the house to open windows and clear out any remaining smoke.

Carl escorted the triplets up to their rooms to assess the damage from the fire. Since Crystal's room was directly under Skip's, and the rooms on either side of his also suffered damage, the girls decided it was wise to gather some things and temporarily move down to the first floor with the rest of the family.

After a thorough assessment of the damage, Carl contacted his insurance company. Then he called a reputable construction business to come out and give him a written estimate on repairs to submit to his insurance company. The sooner he initiated the process, the sooner he could begin restoration of his manor.

Martha and the girls warmly welcomed Skip's family into their home, assigning them first-floor guestrooms and feeding them an elaborate lunch.

"My goodness," exclaimed Erin. "Is this the way you treated Skip?"

"He's a fine young man, Erin," said Martha. "And we thoroughly enjoyed having him. Didn't we, dear?"

"Uh, yeah. We sure did. But I still think he started that fire."

"Carl!"

Doesn't Martha see it? I know that boy did it, even if by accident, and someone has to pay for the damages. "I don't mean to offend anyone, but I intend to question him."

"That's fine," said Erin. "I can't imagine Skip being responsible for something like that, but he'll tell you the truth. He doesn't lie."

"So it doesn't bother you if I ask him?"

"Of course not. Mr. Masterson, any one of us could accidentally start a fire. It only takes a moment of carelessness."

"So you agree that he might have done it."

"Carl!"

Erin sighed. "Mr. Masterson, you believe that Skip is guilty. I'll accept that. If you find proof, or if he admits it, I'll assume full responsibility."

"Good enough," said Carl. *Now all I have to do is get him to admit that he could have caused it.* "You and your girls are welcome to stay."

I don't think so. How could they stay with the man accusing her son of something she knew he didn't do? "No, thank you. We'll get a hotel in town."

"You'll do nothing of the sort," said Martha. "You and these little ones will stay with us. We have more than enough room. It is our fault that Skip is even in the hospital. It is immaterial *how* that fire got started. He came here in aid to our daughters. He rescued Crystal from drowning. We are responsible for him. We owe you all the support we can give you. Now I've arranged for our driver to run you home, dear. Your little girls may stay here while you're gone. Our daughters will love having them."

Martha's concern for Skip and her invitation to stay touched Erin's heart. "Thank you. May I make a quick phone call first?"

Martha directed her to the nearest telephone. Erin phoned Cassandra's mother and explained the situation. After obtaining permission for Cassandra to stay with them, Erin requested that Anita pack her daughter a small suitcase for a few nights away from home.

Skip slept for hours. Sitting on the chair beside his bed, Cassandra held his hand and ran her fingers through his hair.

"Hey, beautiful, what's your name?" The man in the other bed grinned at her.

"Cassandra McKenzie."

"Nice to meet you, Cassandra. May I call you Cassie?"

"If you'd like."

My name's Michael Andrews. I get out of the hospital tomorrow. How 'bout a date? I know this great little restaurant ..."

"No, thanks, Michael. I'm engaged."

"To Shawn?"

"To Skip? Yes."

"I thought his name was Shawn."

"It's a nickname. His first name is Skip."

"Oh. You sure you don't want to go out with me? You're the loveliest creature I've ever laid my eyes on. Besides, he's in the hospital. He'll never know."

Cassandra studied Skip, stroking his cheek, aware that Michael watched her.

"Cassie?"

He's adorable. She fingered Skip's hair. *He's so cute when he's asleep.*

"Just one little date?" begged Michael. "Please, Cassie. Just say *yes.*"

"No, Michael. I love Skip."

"Yeah, but does he love you? The other day, I caught him kissing Crystal down by the swimming pool."

With a gasp, Cassandra jerked back like an electric jolt shot through her.

"And we caught him in Crystal's room. He was dressed in pajamas, and everyone saw them come out together."

"He was in her room wearing pajamas?"

Michael grinned. "Crystal still denies that anything is going on between them."

Cassandra gazed at Skip with a frown. Crystal did deny it, but the girl was kind and tender. She expressed genuine concern for him. Cassandra suspected that there was something that Michael wasn't telling her. Caressing Skip's face, she cupped his chin and kissed him. "We're engaged to be married."

"Unfortunately, he doesn't remember. He's had a severe case of amnesia and doesn't even know you."

"Yes, he does. He called me by name when he saw me."

"He did?"

"Yes. You may as well drop it, Michael, because I won't go out with you." A sudden thought hit her. *Drop it.* That was the same thing Crystal told him. Was there a reason that Michael wouldn't drop it? Did something happen between them? Now Cassandra wondered, and she would definitely ask Skip about it.

"There's nothing I could do to persuade you to change your mind?" asked Michael.

"I'm afraid not."

Erin learned that the triplets had a massive gym set in the immaculately finished cellar of their huge home, and that's where the girls ran to play, allowing her to slip off by herself.

Carl's driver, Grant, amiably chatted with her the entire drive. He described the way Skip's presence warmed the entire household, the fistfight between him and Michael and how her son took down three of them single-handedly before running off. He learned from Devon, who got it from the girls, that Carl sent the police after him, and it took the entire police department to catch him.

Erin laughed at Grant's vocal expression and the amusing way he shared the situations. Yet, she couldn't envision her son running from the police, but it pleased her that he returned to the Masterson estate willingly.

Finally, Grant explained how the newspaper article proclaimed Skip's engagement to Carl's daughter and that it brought dozens of gold diggers to the door, all claiming relation to Skip in order to cash in on his promised inheritance. Now she understood why they required proof that she was his mother.

Having amnesia, in a state of innocence, her precious son would have gone with anyone, and Carl Masterson prevented that from happening. For that, Erin would always be grateful. Yet, the man who worked so hard to protect her son now accused him.

Chapter 32

A Forced Confession

Grant's amusing tales entertained Erin for the duration of the drive. When they arrived at her Forest Valley home fewer than two hours later, she threw together a couple of suitcases for herself and the girls. Knowing that everything Skip had taken with him on his assignment had likely been lost in the fire, she packed essentials for him, as well.

Grant hauled the suitcases out to the car and set them in the trunk. Then they headed across town to Cassandra's house, picked up her suitcase, and jumped on the road out of town, returning to the Masterson estate shortly after 5:00. Erin found her young daughters anxiously awaiting her return.

"Mom, can we go to the ho'pital and see Skip now?" asked Suzi.

"Absolutely."

Before they left, Carl instructed Devon regarding dinner and told Grant where to place the suitcases.

Driven by the need to assign blame for the fire, Carl accompanied Erin and her daughters to the hospital.

Great! The boy was still asleep. Carl was anxious to interrogate him about starting that fire, but he had no intentions of interrupting this family reunion, especially after all the trouble he went through to reunite Skip with his family.

The young girls gathered around his bed.

"Skip?" Seven-year-old Sandy shook him. "Wake up."

Little Suzi kissed his cheek while the youngest crawled onto his bed and lay her head on his chest. Skip wrapped his right arm around her.

"Skip's awake!" exclaimed Suzi, leaping onto his bed

Cassandra snatched her up. "No, no, Suzi. He has an IV in his arm." With a hug, she set the child on the floor. "We need to be gentle with him right now."

"OK."

Skip grimaced and turned his head. His sisters kissed him repeatedly.

"They've missed you, sweetheart," said his mother.

"I can tell. They're bombarding me with three weeks' worth of kisses."

"How do you feel, Skip?" asked Cassandra.

"I hurt." His voice was raspy and hoarse.

Carl could tell that it was a strain for him to talk.

Cassandra rested her hand on Skip's. "Was anything going on between you and Crystal?"

"No. Why?"

"Michael said he caught you two kissing by the pool."

"That doesn't surprise me."

"Did you?"

Skip jumped at her accusatory tone of voice.

Carl shot Michael a look of irritation, displeased with him for telling tales that would create friction between Skip and Cassandra.

Michael grinned.

"Well?" Cassandra's tone demanded an answer.

Tension permeated the hospital room with silence.

"No," he whispered.

"Then why would he say such a thing if it weren't true?"

Carl raised an eyebrow. She was about to crucify him on lies. Didn't Cassandra know him well enough by now to trust his character?

"'Cause he's a liar," rasped Skip. "Cassie, I love you. I'm not interested in any other girls, so don't listen to anything that Michael says."

"Were you in Crystal's bedroom in pajamas?"

"I don't know. My memories of that first night are awfully vague."

Cassandra looked at Carl for confirmation, and he nodded. Her expression softened. Sliding her fingers down his arm, she grasped his hand. "I really missed you."

Settled in an armchair, Carl quietly watched the joyful reunion between Skip and his family. Obviously the only boy in a houseful of girls, the lad easily accepted the tenderness of their constant touch. As the little ones started to get restless and hungry, Carl rose from his chair. He'd waited an hour to question Skip, and it was now his turn.

"We need to go," said Cassandra. "The girls are getting hungry. See you tomorrow, Skip." Cassandra squeezed his hand and ushered the little ones out the door.

Erin's gaze shifted from the girls filing out of the room to her son, and Carl knew that she wasn't ready to leave his side. Regardless, he needed to talk to Skip, and no time was better than right now.

Carl cleared his throat. "Mrs. Shaughnessy, may I speak with Skip for a minute?"

A look of dread crossed her face.

"Alone."

Skip grasped his mother's hand, straining to talk. "Mom, it's OK."

"Sweetheart, do you want to talk to him?"

"Yeah, Mom, Mr. Masterson has been real kind to me. Don't be angry with him for what happened. It wasn't his fault."

Tears slid down Erin's cheeks, and she squeezed his hand. "I know it wasn't, son. I'll wait in the hall."

Erin left his room and quietly closed the door behind her.

Finally! With pursed lips, Carl leaned against the bed rail. "Son, what's your name?" He gazed absently out the window.

"Skip Shaughnessy."

"How old are you, Skip?"

"I'm nineteen, sir."

"Where do you work?"

"Forest Valley Police Department." The lad spoke barely above a whisper.

Pushing away from Skip's bed, Carl started pacing. "How come you didn't tell me this before? That first night at my house, I asked you for your name and age, or don't you remember?"

"Yes, sir, I do, but ..."

Carl jerked to a stop and glared at him. "Then why didn't you tell me?"

Skip jumped at his tone of voice. "Be ... be ... because I couldn't remember them."

"Do you remember what happened to you or how you even got into our house?"

"N-n-no, sir." Skip's voice quivered. "I only know what you told me."

Carl looked away. "Fair enough. Do you know what happened this morning?"

"No, sir."

Carl had a hard time believing that. Skip was in that room. He had to know *something*. "How did that fire start, Skip?"

"I don't know."

His continual denial assured Carl of the boy's guilt. Now all he needed was a confession. "Did you start it?"

"No, sir. I would never start a fire."

"Then tell me what happened."

Skip paused. "I don't know."

Carl frowned. "Sounds like a case of selective amnesia. And you don't remember anything at all?"

"I remember getting hit."

"By whom?"

"Michael."

"Come on, Skip. You could whip Michael blindfolded, so don't try to pin this on him. Now I want to know how that fire got started."

"I don't know!" exclaimed Skip, straining his voice to speak above a whisper.

"And you haven't got a clue as to what happened? You know that the fire originated in your room, don't you?"

Skip gasped. "It did?"

"Yes, it did. If you don't remember what happened, how do you know that you didn't have something to do with it?"

Skip was speechless.

"Well? How do you?" demanded Carl.

"I don't," rasped Skip.

"That's exactly right. You don't. You couldn't even remember your name and age. Is it possible that you had something to do with that fire and just don't remember?"

Skip swallowed hard. Carl knew that he wanted to say *no,* but how could he when he claimed to have no idea what had happened?

"Well?" yelled Carl.

"Yes, sir, it is."

"Good. That's what I wanted to hear you say. Now, tell *that* to your mother."

Chapter 33

Trouble on the Horizon

Michael caught his breath. *No! Skip didn't do it. Why doesn't he fight the charge?*

Carl swung open the door and motioned for Erin to enter. "He has something to tell you."

He helped me out of that burning building, or I might still be sitting there. After everything I did to him, he came to my aid. And this is how I repay him? By allowing him to take the rap for my stupidity? That's not right.

Erin crossed the room to her son's bedside. "Skip, did you have something to do with that fire?"

Michael cringed. *So when have I ever done what was right? I could have paid for my nephew's open-heart surgery, but I didn't. Why should I start doing the right thing now?*

"I guess I might have. I don't know what happened."

This is different. Michael felt greatly conflicted. *No, it's not. Misty protected me from dad's fury by keeping her whereabouts secret. He would have beaten me to a pulp to get it out of me. I owe her for that. And Shawn helped me today. I owe him.*

With a frown, Carl jammed his hands in his pockets, glancing out the window and back at Skip. "I'm sorry to do that to you, Skip. You're a fine young man, but all the evidence points to you, whether or not you remember what happened. And somebody has to pay for the damage."

"Leave him alone, Carl. He didn't do it." Sudden fear engulfed Michael. *My gosh! Did I just say that?*

"Oh? And how would you know that?" demanded Carl.

Michael tensed. To answer that question meant a confession, and he wasn't certain he was ready for the consequences. Carl's temper would flare hotter than the fire.

"What were you doing in our house at that hour?"

"I told you. I came to apologize to Crystal."

"That's what you told me, all right. Just like you told Cassandra that you caught Skip kissing Crystal by the pool. Now, tell me the truth!"

I'm doomed. He sees right through me. "Um ... I ..."

Stepping over to Skip's hospital bed, Carl examined him. "Skip said that you hit him. I should have paid more attention to the bruises on his face – bruises that he didn't have last night when he went to bed."

Michael swallowed hard. "I ... I'm sorry. I didn't mean to hit him so hard, but I was angry."

"Why did you hit him at all? You lied to me!" Carl glared at him from across the room. "Now, what were you doing in our house at that hour?"

Michael didn't answer.

Carl started toward him. "You were in Skip's room while he was sleeping. Weren't you? That's why he doesn't know what happened."

Michael shook his head. "No! I wasn't."

"Then tell me how you managed to beat him up. You don't know how to fight, and Skip is trained in self-defense."

"W-w-well, I ..." Michael grasped the covers so hard, his knuckles turned white.

"How did you escape a single blow? Did you throw the first punch while he was still asleep?"

"Yes!" cried Michael. "I did! Everything you said is true. All right?"

"No, Michael, it is *not* all right! You were in his room! You know how that fire got started!"

"No, I ... I ... I don't."

"Yes, you do! You smoke. Did you have a lit cigarette in that room?"

Michael hedged. "Don't be silly, Carl. You don't permit smoking in the house."

"Answer my question, Michael!"

Michael looked away.

"You set that fire!"

"It was an accident. I set the cigarette on the edge of the dresser. It must have gotten knocked down ..." Michael's voice trailed off.

Erin looked on in stunned silence while Carl digested this new information. "I'll see to it that you go to jail for this, Michael."

"You can't prove I did it!"

Carl's eyes narrowed. "Don't bet on it. In addition, I intend to press charges against you for illegal entry and burglary. By the way, Skip is a cop, so you assaulted a police officer."

Michael's heart nearly stopped. Carl slammed his fist into the palm of his hand, and Michael jumped.

"Don't you ever come back to my house or associate with my family in any way." Spinning on his heel, Carl stormed out.

Skip cringed. His mother grasped his hand, and he pulled her close to whisper in her ear. "Mr. Masterson is a really nice man, but he doesn't know the Lord. See if you can talk to him?"

"I'll try, son. Would you like Cassandra to stay with you?"

"No, ma'am. I need to talk to Michael."

"All right, sweetheart." His mother squeezed his hand and kissed him before hurrying after Carl.

Lying flat on his back, Skip looked at Michael through the bedrail. He wanted to sit up for this discussion, but he hurt too badly to reposition himself. "Why did you admit it?"

With a look of shame, Michael turned away.

"He was convinced that I did it. Had you kept quiet, no one else would have known."

Michael wrung his hands and gazed across the room. "After everything I said and did, you still helped me. That fire was going when I left your room. I could have stamped it out, but I left you there to die."

"Why?" Skip strained to speak above a whisper. "Because you thought there was something going on between me and Crystal?"

"You wouldn't understand!"

"You're right. I don't. A relationship must be cultivated by trust."

Michael looked at him. "And how much do you trust your girlfriend?"

"A lot. And she's much more than my girlfriend. She's my fiancée."

"Is that a fact? Well, we've got a date for tomorrow night."

"Have a good time."

Michael's eyes widened. "Huh? You're not mad?"

"Getting angry wouldn't solve anything. I don't believe you anyway. But if it were true, I would call off our engagement."

"You wouldn't fight for her?" asked Michael.

"Of course, I would. But I'm not fighting over her. She committed herself to me when she accepted my wedding proposal, but if you steal her from me, you can have her."

"You're joking. Right?"

"Michael, if you're able to entice her away from me, then I never really had her heart to begin with. I'd rather let her go now, then end up later in divorce court. Marriage is for life, and I'm choosing my life partner with care."

"You're different from any guy I've ever talked to. I've never heard it put that way before."

"Now, do you want to tell me the truth about you and Cassandra?"

Michael sighed. "I asked her out, but she turned me down. She was only interested in you. I can't get over how much the girls love you. What makes you so different?"

"I gave my life to Jesus," said Skip.

"Is that it? Religion makes that much difference?"

"Not religion. Christ."

"What's the difference?"

"Religion is man's feeble attempt to reach God. Jesus said, 'No man cometh to the Father but by me.' Christ died on the cross to pay the penalty for your sins. All you have to do is accept the payment."

"That sounds too easy," said Michael.

"It is easy. God made it easy so everyone could get to Him."

"How come you came to my aid after what I did to you? I certainly didn't deserve it."

"No, you didn't. But then, I don't deserve God's mercy and forgiveness. My sins nailed His Son to a cross."

"I'm miserable, but you're happy all the time."

"Whatever gave you that idea? It doesn't make me happy to get beat up or accused of something I didn't do or chased by the police or nearly drowned trying to rescue someone. When I woke up surrounded by flames, I was scared to death."

"You were? You seemed so calm and confident."

"The Bible says, 'The Lord is my refuge and strength; a very present help in time of trouble.' And boy was I in trouble. But God is gracious and merciful. He spared my life."

"Skip, how do I give my life to Jesus?"

"Acts 16:31says 'Believe on the Lord Jesus Christ and thou shalt be saved.'"

"That's all there is to it? Just believe?"

"And Romans 10:13 says 'For whosoever shall call upon the name of the Lord shall be saved.'"

"How do I do that?" asked Michael.

"Pray. Bow your head and close your eyes and talk to God just like you talk to me. Tell Him that you know you're a sinner and that you can't save yourself. Then ask Him to come into your heart and life and be your Savior."

"That's all I do?"

"And believe."

"Well, I want whatever-it-is that makes you so kind and forgiving." Michael bowed his head and prayed, asking Jesus to be his Savior. With tear-filled eyes, he looked over at Skip. "I'm so sorry for what I did to you. It's my fault that you got burned. Thank you for telling me about Jesus. What can I do to show my appreciation?"

Skip smiled. "Nothing."

"I don't have much time anyway. I'll probably go to jail for what I did."

"Why don't you talk to Mr. Masterson?"

Michael sighed. "He won't listen."

"Maybe not, but what have you got to lose?"

"Skip, you're not really a cop, are you?"

"Yeah."

Michael groaned. "Oh, boy. The penalty for assaulting a police officer is far more severe. Are you going to press charges against me?"

"No."

Michael breathed a sigh of relief. "Thanks. Carl will for certain."

"Talk to him, Michael. Offer to pay for the damages. Show him that you've changed."

"Might as well try. I haven't anything to lose."

Knowing that Michael needed to collect every ounce of courage to face Carl, Skip prayed for him.

Chapter 34

A Plea for Mercy

Erin and Carl rode back to the Masterson manor in silence. She thought it best to give Carl time to cool off. Uncertain what to say or how to proceed, she slipped off by herself before supper to pray and seek God's guidance through His Word.

At supper, Carl ate in silence, an embittered expression marring his features.

Erin studied him with growing uneasiness. How could she talk to him about his need for the Lord when the situation ignited such rage in his heart? But immediately after supper, Carl resolved her dilemma by initiating the conversation.

"Mrs. Shaughnessy, may I talk to you in my office?"

"Certainly." Erin followed him in and quietly sat down on the chair opposite his desk.

Carl dropped into the chair behind his desk and buried his face in his hands. After several long seconds, he folded his hands on his desk and looked at her.

"Ma'am, I owe you an apology for falsely accusing your son. My common sense told me that he didn't do it, but I was so upset that I ... I wanted to blame someone, so I didn't look past the obvious. I'm sorry."

"I appreciate your honesty, Mr. Masterson, but Skip deserves this apology. He's the one you accused."

Carl looked away. "I guess I kind of overlooked that. Didn't I?"

"I'd say so, but it's not too late to give it to him. It's good to hear it, even though he's already forgiven you."

"What about you, Mrs. Shaughnessy?" His voice was soft and pensive, almost fearful.

"Me?" Erin laughed. "Oh, you don't need my forgiveness."

"No. What I really need is your mercy. Because when you find out what he's been through, you'll want to file a lawsuit against me. If this is made public, I'll be ruined. Could we possibly settle quietly, out of court? I'll give you anything you want if you don't go to a lawyer or the papers."

"I have no intentions of bringing suit against you, Mr. Masterson. It would serve no purpose, and I already know what he's been through. Crystal told me that she clobbered him with the car. And while en route to Forest Valley, Grant briefed me on Skip's three-day stay with your lovely family. Grant filled me in on everything, including all you went through trying to protect him while you attempted to locate us. For that, I'm truly grateful."

With a grin, Carl rubbed his chin and leaned back in his chair. "Ma'am, if there were any doubt in my mind that you are really his mother, you've just removed it. You are too kind."

"Thank you, Mr. Masterson. It's my desire to serve the Lord."

"Serve the Lord?" Carl raised an eyebrow. "How is this serving the Lord?"

"The Bible says to let your light so shine before men that they see your good works and glorify your Father which is in Heaven. Crystal did not intentionally hit Skip with the car, and you had no control over that fire."

"That's for sure."

"And despite your best effort to protect him, he still got beat up. What happened to Skip was beyond your control."

"I'm sorry. I don't know what else to say."

"There's nothing to say. Skip's right. None of this is your fault."

"Skip doesn't blame me for any of it?"

"You mean, like you blamed him for starting that fire? No."

"I really do owe him an apology." Carl bounded to his feet. "Excuse me, Mrs. Shaughnessy. I have to run to the hospital." He strode out the office door.

Troubled by his own stupidity and the mess he'd gotten himself into, Michael glanced over at Skip. "Carl is going to kill me. What can I do, Skip? How can I get him to calm down enough to listen to what I have to say? How? I've never seen him so angry."

"Pray, Michael."

Michael shuddered. "I doubt even God could do anything. Carl has the worst temper of anyone I've ever met." Michael wrung his hands and stared at the wall. "He'll be back. I know he will. When he gets here, will you talk to him for me? Try to calm him down and smooth things over. Please, Skip. He'll listen to you."

Skip yawned. "I'll try."

Just then, the door opened and the nurse entered. "Supper time. You fellows hungry?"

Michael shook his head. "I can't eat right now. My stomach is tied up in knots."

The nurse pushed a cart over to Skip's bed and raised the head of his bed so he could eat. "Well, I know you're hungry. You slept through lunch. How do you feel?"

"I hurt."

She set his dinner tray in front of him. "Here's some pain medication." She offered him a little cup with two tablets in it. "It will greatly reduce your discomfort." The nurse tipped the tablets into his hand and handed him a cup of water.

Skip downed the tablets.

"Now that might make you sleepy." The nurse replaced his IV bag with a new one.

"Oh, no. I wish you had told me that before I took them. I want to be alert when my fiancée comes to see me."

The nurse smiled at him and set a meal tray on Michael's bedside tray table before leaving the room. Constantly glancing over at Skip, Michael toyed distractedly with his food. Skip finished his supper, pushed away his tray, and lowered his bed. Within a minute, he was asleep.

"Skip?" Michael desperately wanted someone to talk to him.

The door opened, and Carl strode in. He stopped short when he saw that Skip was asleep.

Michael swallowed a lump. "Carl, may I have a moment of your precious time?"

Carl glared at him. "I came to see Skip."

"Please, sir. I know that you're angry, and you have every right to be, but please hear me out."

"You have exactly sixty seconds to say your piece." Carl glanced at his watch.

Michael gulped down a breath of air. "I started that fire. I accept financial responsibility for all repairs and replacement of damaged property."

"Your admission of guilt will not reduce your jail time by one day. I intend to press charges against you for every offense I can."

"Please don't press charges against me. I'll pay for every bit of damage, but I don't want to go to jail."

"You should have thought of that before you entered our house illegally and assaulted Skip."

"Skip's not pressing charges against me."

"He should. I'll talk to him about it."

"No, Carl, please don't."

Without replying, Carl marched out the door, letting it swing shut behind him.

His vision blurred by tears, Michael bit his lower lip and gazed across the room at Skip. Despite their loud discussion, his sleeping roommate didn't stir.

Michael choked down a lump and looked from the closed door to the silent telephone. He had no one to turn to, no one to talk to. Carl was a powerfully persuasive man who easily influenced others to his way of thinking. And after the way Michael had mistreated Skip, it wouldn't take much to sway his decision.

Michael looked upward. "Jesus, are you there? Do you answer prayer like Skip says you do? Because I need a miracle."

A Real Friend

With a heavy heart and a downtrodden spirit, intense fear and overwhelming anxiety settled into Michael's very being. And for the first time in his adult life, his money couldn't redeem him from trouble.

The hospital room door swung open and Cassandra entered, followed by the triplets. The girls gathered around Skip. Resting her hand on his head, Cassandra fingered his blond hair. Michael gazed at her intently.

Cassandra caught him staring at her and blushed. "What's the matter?"

"That Skip's a lucky guy to have a girl like you." He glanced at Crystal and back at Cassandra. "An awfully lucky guy."

"I'm the lucky one. Skip's kindness and easy-going temperament draw girls like a magnet, yet he chose me. He's my best friend."

The girls talked softly among themselves, no longer including him in their discussion. Michael watched Cassandra caress Skip.

Crystal never touches me like that.

Skip slept through their visit. An hour after the girls arrived, the nurse poked her head in the door and announced that visiting hours were over.

"But we didn't get to see him," said Billie. "He slept the whole time."

"I'm sorry, girls. Hospital rules. You may come back tomorrow when he's awake."

The girls started toward the door.

"Bye, Crystal," said Michael.

Crystal tossed him a wave before following her sisters out the door.

She didn't even glance in my direction. They only care about Skip. Michael swallowed hard and gazed at his sleeping roommate. "Skip, wake up and talk to me. You're the only one who will."

Michael waited, hoping for a response, but silence permeated the room. As time crept by, Michael rolled and tossed, unable to relax, frequently peering over at Skip to see if he were stirring.

Around sunrise, Skip started to get restless, turning from side to side and kicking down his covers. "No!" He shook his head. *"Put down that gun! Now!"*

Michael sat up and looked across the room at him.

"I said, put it down!" cried Skip. "Drop it, or I'll shoot."

Michael slid off the bed and grabbed his crutches. Hobbling across the room, he lowered the side rail on Skip's bed and plopped down beside him.

Awakened with a start, Skip jumped. He instinctively drew in a sharp breath and shielded his face with his arms.

Michael gently touched his arm. "Hey, are you OK? You were yelling in your sleep."

"I was?" Skip rubbed the sleep from his eyes. "What a nightmare, I was having. Thanks for waking me."

Michael bit his lower lip. He had never felt so alone in his whole life, and he desperately needed someone to talk to.

"Skip, you're the only friend I have. Carl intends to bring charges against me. I promised to pay for the damage, but he wants revenge. Please don't turn on me. I'll do anything to make it up to you."

"Michael, I told you that I wouldn't press charges. Don't you believe me?" Skip's voice was much stronger, and the hoarseness was nearly gone.

"Yes, but Carl Masterson is a persuasive man, and he promised to sway your decision against me."

"The man who falsely accused me? I don't think so. Now, go back to bed and get some sleep."

"I can't sleep. My stomach is tied up in knots. Carl wants me in jail. I'm doomed."

Skip yawned and rubbed his eyes. "I'm sorry I can't help you, but I know Someone who can."

"Who?"

"Jesus. He's only a prayer away. Now that you've trusted Him as your Savior, why don't you talk to Him about your situation?"

"How?"

"I'll show you." Closing his eyes, Skip interceded for Michael in prayer. "Lord Jesus, Michael is worried about going to jail for the things he did before coming to know You. Now that he's your child, he desires to do what is right and pleasing in your sight. Show him Your power. Give him Your peace. Guide and direct him through the circumstances he now faces. And though the consequences may be unpleasant, help him to accept them..."

"Don't pray like that!"

Skip looked at him. "Unfortunately, sin always comes with consequences. God readily forgives us, but the results are still there. The damage caused by the fire won't disappear just because you're sorry for what you did and asked God to forgive you."

"You mean, I may still go to jail?"

"With Mr. Masterson pursuing charges against you, that's a very real possibility, I'm afraid. However, that doesn't mean that God abandoned you, or that He didn't really forgive you. It simply means that you still have to face the consequences of your actions. But Jesus will be with you. He will never leave you, nor forsake you."

Michael blinked back tears and dried his eyes with his hand. "Thanks, Skip. You're a real friend, the kind that I want to be from now on."

Snatching up his crutches, he hobbled back to his own bed. Michael crawled under the covers, and he felt an indescribable peace settle over him moments before he drifted to sleep.

Now wide awake, Skip lay in bed talking to Jesus and thinking of his family. As the sun lightened the room, the nurse strolled in.

"My goodness, you're awake early. How do you feel?"

Skip read her nameplate. "Much better. Thank you, Emily."

Emily drew the curtains and switched on the light.

Skip slapped his hand over his eyes.

"Does the light hurt your eyes, sweetie. I'm sorry. Doctor Cantin is making her morning rounds and will be right in to examine you. Let me remove the dressings on these burns." Emily raised the head of Skip's bed and helped him sit up, slipping off his hospital gown.

"May I exchange that gown for pajamas?"

"I'm not sure that's a good idea, but I'll ask the doctor for you." Emily gently unbandaged his arms and chest where he'd sustained the most serious burns. Her eyes widened.

Just then, a young, female doctor stepped into the curtained partition. "My, aren't you looking good." She pulled off his covers and examined him. "Much better than yesterday. I thought you might need skin grafting. Though we'll have to be careful to prevent infection, I don't think any grafts will be necessary. I have never seen a burn heal so fast."

"I serve a gracious God."

"You believe God did it, huh?"

"Of course. You didn't do it. Did you?"

"No. We sure didn't."

"Well, who else is there?"

Doctor Cantin rolled her eyes.

"If God brought instant healing to people in Bible times, then He can certainly heal me," said Skip.

"Any sensible person knows that the Bible is nothing but religious nonsense, so I hope you don't buy into its validity."

Skip cocked his head. "You don't believe in the Bible?"

"Afraid not. It's nothing but a bunch of fairy tales."

"I'm sorry you feel that way, but your opinion doesn't tarnish its truth," said Skip.

Doctor Cantin shot him an irritated look before turning to Emily. "He's doing remarkably well. Re-wrap these burns."

"Yes, doctor. Also, he'd like to wear pajamas instead of a gown."

"They'll be much harder to get on and off when we need to change the dressing. I'd prefer him to stay in a gown for now." The doctor re-covered Skip and disappeared through the curtain opening, leaving his room.

Emily smiled at Skip. "Sorry."

"I'm not wearing that," said Skip. "Gowns are for girls."

"Maybe we can compromise. Since the burn on your legs is superficial, I'll sneak you a pair of pajama bottoms," said Emily as she carefully re-bandaged him.

"You won't make me wear a gown?"

"No, but I won't bring you a shirt, either. Will pajama bottoms suffice? If not, you'll have to choose between this girly gown or your underwear?"

Skip considered her proposition. He preferred wearing a shirt, but it would be painful maneuvering it off for the nurse and back on again for his own comfort. Yet, in a room full of girls, pajama bottoms would keep him more comfortable than stripped to his underwear. Either way, he wasn't going to wear that gown even one more minute.

"Yes, Ma'am. Pajama bottoms are fine."

"Now tell me about the Bible. I'm interested in learning. Where should I start reading?"

"I'd recommend you start in the Gospel according to John."

"I'll do that," said Emily, clipping the bandage in place. "I can't get over how much better those burns look in such a short time. It's nothing we've done. That's for sure. I wouldn't have believed it if I hadn't seen it. And the Bible chronicles instantaneous healings?"

"Yes, Ma'am."

"I'll start reading it this afternoon as soon as I get home from work."

Carl trotted into the dining room where everyone was seated for breakfast. Kissing his wife, he said, "Don't wait for me this morning. I have some business to tend to." He patted her arm and left the room.

Jumping into his Jeep, Carl raced to the hospital.

First, I'll apologize to Skip for accusing him. I still can't believe I did that. What was I thinking? And Michael was there before breakfast. That should have told me that he wasn't there to see Crystal, let alone apologize to her. He doesn't understand the meaning of the word.

When he entered Skip's room, he found Skip playing checkers with the nurse. Carl strolled through the door in time to see the nurse jump his last checker.

With a smile, the nurse collected the checkers and board. "Good game," she said. "You put up quite a fight and almost beat me that time. I'll be back later, and we'll play another game. I have to give you an opportunity for a rematch." Exiting his room, she softly shut the door.

"Sounds like you lost them all," said Carl. "Do you ever win at checkers? The girls said that they've beaten you every game."

Skip smiled. "I win when I want to win."

Carl raised an eyebrow. "You mean, you let her win?"

"No, sir. I never purposely throw a game of checkers, but winning isn't usually important to me. I play to have fun and build relationships."

"Son, you're incredible. And I owe you an apology."

272

"Thank you, sir. Your apology is accepted."

Carl glanced over at Michael and back at Skip.

"He had a restless night," said Skip. "He didn't finally fall asleep until nearly six this morning."

"Well, I hope he enjoys it, because tomorrow he'll be sleeping behind bars. I'll see to that, and I want you to help me. You're in the hospital because of him."

"God is merciful. I could be dead."

"Indeed you could. He assaulted you and left you unconscious in a burning building. That's how you got burned. Isn't it?"

"Yes, sir. And Crystal nearly killed me with the car."

Chapter 36

Accepting the Payment

Carl pursed his lips in frustration. Now Skip had *him* on the defensive, and he didn't like it one bit. He crammed his hands in his pockets and looked away. "That was different. She didn't do it on purpose."

"It was carelessness, just like the fire Michael started."

Carl narrowed his eyes and turned on Skip. "It never should have happened. He had no business in my house in the first place."

"I agree, but your girls are just as guilty. JJ and Billie borrowed your car without permission and got stranded. I brought them home. Then Crystal recklessly took off in search of them and nearly killed someone."

"She panicked, whereas Michael intentionally attacked you."

"That's true, but he didn't intend to start a fire. He was somewhere he shouldn't have been, like JJ and Billie, and he got reckless, like Crystal. Then he got scared and ran instead of smothering the fire while it was small. Your daughters did the same thing. Just like Michael, they didn't admit what they had done until you cornered them. They tried to keep you from knowing how their actions demolished two cars and injured a stranger. Had JJ and Billie stayed home, none of this would have happened. I stopped to change their flat tire."

"So you're blaming my daughters?" demanded Carl.

"I'm not blaming anyone, sir. But can't you see that Michael's actions were no different than that of your daughters. I simply got caught in the middle."

Swallowing a lump, Carl strolled over to look out the window. Silence saturated the room. Without shifting his gaze, his fists on his hips, Carl cleared his throat. "Skip, Michael says that you're not pressing charges against him. Is that true?"

"Yes, sir."

"Why not?"

"It would serve no purpose, Mr. Masterson."

Carl spun toward him. "After what he did to you, he deserves everything he has coming to him."

"I agree. But God was merciful to me when I didn't deserve it."

"What do you mean by that?"

Skip glanced over at his sleeping roommate, then up at Carl. "Even at my very best, I fail. The Bible says that my righteousness is as filthy rags."

"That's nonsense."

"Is it now? Tell me why you want to send your future son-in-law to jail."

"He's no longer my future son-in-law. I won't let any of my girls marry a beast like him." Carl started pacing. "He's deceitful and dishonest, full of rage and jealousy. I'm glad you came, Skip. Having you around revealed the kind of animal he really is. I'd like all my daughters to marry boys like you."

"Mr. Masterson, you're comparing him with me."

"So? What's wrong with that?"

"Nothing, sir, but before I came you weren't comparing him with anyone. That raised your expectations of his behavior, and he resented it. Just like you resent God for maintaining perfect standards."

Carl jerked to a stop and waved his hand through the air. "I can't live up to God's standards!"

"No one can," said Skip. "We all sin. And the wages of sin is death. God created us to have fellowship with Him, but sin can't enter into His presence. So in order to reconcile us to Himself, He came to Earth in the form of a man. Then he died on the cross to pay the penalty for our sin. All we have to do is accept the payment."

"I can't believe that's all there is to it. There must be more."

"Mr. Masterson, did Michael offer to pay for the damage to your estate?"

"Yeah."

"Did you accept his offer of payment?"

Shuffling his feet, Carl looked away. "No."

"Then who's going to have to pay for it?"

"I will."

"Well, Jesus paid the penalty for your sin. If you don't accept His payment, who will have to pay for it?"

Carl gasped. "Oh, my goodness. I will!"

"Only that debt is so big and so deep that you'll be separated from God for all eternity in a lake of fire. Why don't you accept His offer of payment while it's still available."

Carl slowly sat on the bed beside Skip. "I don't know how."

"The Bible says 'For whosoever shall call upon the name of the Lord shall be saved.'"

Together, they bowed their heads and prayed. Carl confessed that he was a sinner and couldn't save himself. Then he asked Jesus to forgive and save him.

"Thanks, Skip."

"You're welcome, sir. Now when Michael wakes up, see if his offer of payment is still available. I'm certain it will be."

A rattling door caught Carl's attention, and he looked over at the two young men who entered, wearing blue jeans and short-sleeve, collared shirts.

"Mind if we come in? I'm Tim Brock, and this is Danny McKullen. We stopped by to see how you're doing." They both shook hands with Skip.

Skip greeted them with a smile.

Recognizing their names, Carl slowly rose to his feet, eyeing them curiously. *These are the boys that JJ and Billie were dating.*

"You look much better than you did yesterday when we brought you in," said Tim.

"I feel much better."

Danny grinned. "We asked everyone from our Bible study group to drop what they were doing and pray for you."

"Thanks."

"And we'll continue to pray for you until you're completely well," said Tim. "By the way, Skip, if you had died in that fire, where would you be right now?"

"In heaven, with my Savior and my dad."

Carl raised an eyebrow. Skip was fatherless?

"Your dad's in heaven?" asked Danny.

Skip nodded. "With Jesus. And as much as I miss him, I'm not ready to join him."

The boys laughed.

"We're not ready to go, either," said Danny. "Got to run." With a wave, they headed out the door.

Carl studied them in silence. When they were gone, he let out a soft whistle. "So those are the lads that JJ and Billie are so crazy about." He looked from the empty doorway to Michael, then over at Skip. "Maybe I was a little hasty in my decision to sever their relationships with those two fellows."

"You know them?" asked Skip.

"Not really. I know of them. I don't think they recognized me, though. For once, I'm glad I wasn't recognized."

"That was thoughtful of them to come see me," said Skip.

"Yes, it was," agreed Carl. "Maybe the girls will let me attend their Bible study."

Michael slowly sat up in bed. "I would like to go, too."

Narrowing his eyes, Carl stared at him. Although no longer driven to pursue charges, he had no desire to associate with him, either. "I suppose we can tolerate you for a short while."

Michael's eyes widened. "Does that mean you're not pressing charges against me?"

"Not if you pay for the damages."

"One hundred percent. Skip, you're incredible. You influenced Carl. Thank you."

"God did it, Michael."

Clasping his hands, Michael looked upward. "Thank you, Lord."

Carl raised an eyebrow. "Michael, what's gotten into you? I didn't think you even knew those words."

"I asked Jesus into my life."

"You did?" exclaimed Carl. "When was this?"

"Last night. Carl, I'm sorry for the problems I've caused. Please forgive me."

Carl grinned and winked at Skip. "After Jesus has forgiven me, how can I do less?"

Just then, the door burst open, and Skip's little sisters raced in. Scooter and Suzi scrambled onto the bed and into his lap, Sandy and Stephanie close on their heels.

Skip!" they chorused. The girls flung their arms around him, hugging and kissing him.

Skip grimaced and squeezed his eyes shut. Cassandra and the triplets leaped to his rescue, pulling his sisters off him.

Michael watched the joyous family reunion, feeling like an outsider. While the others chattered excitedly, Emily entered the room with the doctor, who was making his morning rounds. Drawing the curtains, he examined Michael, listening to his lungs with a stethoscope.

"Your lungs sound clear. I'll write up your discharge orders." Pushing aside the curtain, the doctor left the room.

"I'll be back in a little bit with your discharge paperwork," said Emily.

"Take your time. I'm in no hurry." Michael gazed longingly at the crowd of people around Skip. As lonely as he felt here, he didn't relish going home to an empty house.

For an hour, Michael watched the warm interaction and fun-loving bantering between Skip, his family, and the Mastersons. No one spoke to him.

Finally, Emily returned with his discharge paperwork and handed it to him, giving him instructions.

"You're free to go," she said. "I've notified transportation, so they'll be up soon with a wheelchair for you."

Emily left, and Michael drew the curtain that divided the hospital room, changing to go home. He dressed in the only clothes he had with him – ones reeking with the smell of smoke. He intended to shower and change when he got home. With no desire to ride out in a wheelchair, he decided not to wait for transportation. Positioning his crutches under his arms, Michael pushed the curtains aside and hobbled over to Skip.

"Are you leaving?" asked Skip.

Now the center of attention, Michael offered Skip his hand. "Yeah, but I wanted to thank you for being my friend."

Skip shook his hand. "You're welcome, Michael. God bless you. Take care and remember, you have a new Friend who will never leave you nor forsake you. His name is Jesus."

"Thanks, Skip. I'll remember that." Michael looked at Carl. "I'll be in touch with you regarding the damage to your property."

Turning to leave, he spotted Crystal. "Bye, Crystal. I'm sorry for hurting you. I'd like to be your friend, if you'll have me."

"Michael, what's gotten into you? You sound so ... so ... so different."

"I asked Jesus into my heart." Tottering on the crutches, he headed out the door.

"Crystal sprinted after him. "Michael, how are you getting home? Is someone coming to get you?"

"I'll call a cab." Without waiting for a reply, he hobbled out the door.

Crystal turned to her father. "Dad, may I run him home? It won't take me nearly as long as it will for a cab to get here."

Carl tossed her the car keys. "Sure, darling. Take your time."

"Thanks, Dad. I won't be long." Crystal hurried out the door after Michael.

Skip grinned. Crystal had a tender and forgiving heart. And since Michael asked Jesus into his heart, everyone could see a difference in his attitude.

The truth of the gospel had freed Michael from his anger, bitterness, and hostility. And it set him on the straight and narrow path that leads to heaven. Carl, too.

It was only a matter of time before Michael and Crystal were drawn to each other. And Carl would likely bless their union. He hoped they remembered to send him an invitation to their wedding.

A Note from the Author

I started writing about Skip in the early 1990's. I developed an entire novel around the radio call "Officer Down." That was Book One, entitled *Skip Shaughnessy in Keeping Secrets.*

As a firm believer in the Lord Jesus Christ, I find it important to bring my faith into everything I write. Because Jesus is a very real part of my day to day life, I can't separate my love for God from my writing, my stories, and my books.

It took me years to develop Skip's character. He has a desire to please the Lord in all he does. He's a witness and a testimony to the Lord Jesus Christ. He takes opportunities to share the Gospel and he can't help but influence others for good and touch the lives of people everywhere he goes.

As a young mother, when the kids were finally in bed for the night, I'd sit down at my computer and lose myself in a world of make believe that I created. I wrote one novel-length story after another about Skip. I fell in love with him.

And I've known for a long time that God wanted me to get this series published.

It's very hard to land a contract with a mainstream publisher. But today, self-publishing turns dreams into reality. I know that my Lord and Savior is greatly pleased that I'm finally getting these books published and making them available for others to enjoy.

I titled my series "Skip's Action Series." I hope you learn to love him as much as I do.

Preview of Book Three

Skip Shaughnessy in A Way to Escape

He loves her. She loves him. But someone will stop at nothing to separate them. *Permanently!*

Other Books Written by Marjorie Strebe

Skip Shaughnessy in Keeping Secrets
Book 1

When a rookie cop apprehends the drug dealer he believes is responsible for his dad's death, he's targeted by a drug gang who wants him dead, and he starts to fall in love with the adoring young girl who's father pulled the trigger.

Treasures in My Spiritual Hope Chest -

A King James devotional book with scripturally-sound lessons to help you grow spiritually when you read,  understand, and apply God's Word to your life. You will discover priceless nuggets of God's truth in each devotional.

Another, Day, Another Challenge: The Biography of a Child with Williams Syndrome
(Third Edition)

A special needs child with a mental handicap and developmental delays is falling through the cracks of every service designed to support her needs.

For more information, visit www.marjiestrebe.com or email me at kjvwriter@marjiestrebe.com.